"A wife would be—" he hesitated for a moment "—a desirable thing to have."

"Figuratively speaking," Laura murmured.

He looked at her steadily. He didn't move or make any attempt to touch her.

"No, Laura. Not figuratively speaking."

She stared at him.

"I didn't realize that you were talking about…a real marriage. A marriage kind of marriage."

"Is that so unimaginable between you and me?"

Dear Reader,

Happy Valentine's Day! Your response to our FABULOUS FATHERS has been tremendous, so our very special valentine to you is the start of our SUPER FABULOUS FATHERS—larger-than-life super dads who make super husbands! And Barbara McMahon's *Sheik Daddy* is just that. Years ago, gorgeous Ben Shalik had loved Megan O'Sullivan with all his heart, then disappeared, leaving her with a baby girl he never knew existed. And now, the royal daddy was back.... Look for more SUPER FABULOUS FATHERS throughout the year.

To celebrate the most romantic day of the year all month long, we're proud to present VALENTINE BRIDES. Reader favorite, author Phyllis Halldorson starts off the series with *Mail Order Wife*, which is exactly what confirmed bachelor Jim Buckley finds waiting on his doorstep! Christine Scott's *Cinderella Bride* proves that fairy tales can come true when Cynthia Gilbert reluctantly says "I do" to a marriage of convenience. In *The Husband Hunt* by Linda Lewis, Sarah Brannan's after a groom, but the man she's in love with proposes to be something *entirely* different.

You won't want to miss our other VALENTINE BRIDES—*Make-Believe Mom* by Elizabeth Sites and *Going to the Chapel* by Alice Sharpe. Because when Cupid strikes—marriage is sure to follow!

Happy Reading!

Melissa Senate
Senior Editor

Please address questions and book requests to:
Silhouette Reader Service
U.S.: 3010 Walden Ave., P.O. Box 1325, Buffalo, NY 14269
Canadian: P.O. Box 609, Fort Erie, Ont. L2A 5X3

MAKE-BELIEVE MOM

Elizabeth Sites

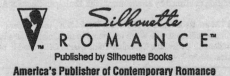

Silhouette
ROMANCE™

Published by Silhouette Books
America's Publisher of Contemporary Romance

Remembering Bob.

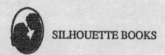

SILHOUETTE BOOKS

ISBN 0-373-19136-7

MAKE-BELIEVE MOM

This edition published by arrangement with Harlequin Books S.A.

Printed in U.S.A.

Books by Elizabeth Sites

Silhouette Romance

The Man Who Changed Everything #1059
Stranger in Her Arms #1094
Make-Believe Mom #1136

ELIZABETH SITES

was born and grew up in Rockford, Illinois. She has moved twenty-nine times in her life, to and from places including New Mexico, New Orleans, the Texas panhandle, North Carolina, the suburbs of Chicago, Austin and her present home in Dallas. She started writing stories in the fourth grade, although for purely practical reasons she has also worked as a proofreader, secretary, radio and television copywriter and producer, respiratory therapist, department store advertising director, radio network vice president, business librarian, magazine editor and marketing consultant. She presently tutors students in English at a private high school.

Dear Reader,

Sometimes the best valentine is the least expected.

It was the eighties, and people were using words like *productivity* and *leverage* and *marketing-driven.* I was dressing for success and I'd almost lost track of who I really was.

He had blue eyes and a beautiful voice and he loved the lush tunes of the thirties and forties and he saw through me as if I were glass.

How did he make it such a memorable Valentine's Day?

Well, he didn't send me red roses. He didn't give me chocolates in a heart-shaped box or a card trimmed with lace. He didn't pop open a bottle of champagne. He was out of town. Business, of course. And I was so wrapped up in my own work that I didn't even think about it. I had forgotten that it was Valentine's Day at all.

He hadn't. And although it had been a grueling trip and his flight was late and any sane practical person would have gone home and collapsed and ordered up the card-roses-candy-champagne in the morning, he rang my buzzer at two in the morning. He had nothing but himself but it didn't matter. Once I got over the shock we sat at the kitchen table and talked and drank coffee that tasted of cinnamon out of two perfectly ordinary mugs and it was one of the most extraordinary nights of my life.

I still have the mugs: plain unromantic gray stoneware with sketchy brush-stroke flowers. Not a heart or a cupid or a frill of lace in sight. But sometimes the very best valentine is indeed the last thing you expect it to be.

Elizabeth Sites

Chapter One

Laura was halfway through her presentation on table settings for springtime dinner parties when the dark man threw open the door to the Driskill's pink-and-white banquet room as if he had every right in the world to be there.

The door struck the wall behind it with a crack like a gunshot. Laura broke off, midsentence. Her after-lunch audience gasped and rustled and craned to look.

The first thing anyone would notice about him was his height. Then there were the hard outdoorsman's muscles in his shoulders and arms that even the discreetest of charcoal gray business tailoring couldn't quite disguise. His straight heavy hair was black and his eyes were black and his face was no stranger to sun and wind. All of a sudden the banquet room seemed smaller and paler and almost suffocatingly feminine.

Laura put down the sterling silver soupspoon she was holding. The ladies of the Maria Brown Austin Philanthropic and Social League leaned forward and whispered to one another behind their ringed and manicured hands.

"...mean you don't know who *that* is?" Laura heard one of the women murmur. "It's Nick Rafland, of all people. The Black Moon ranch. The Rafland Group. Venture capital, you know, and he seems to have this uncanny knack for picking companies that..."

"...his brother." It was another voice. "A week or two after Christmas, on the highway between Austin and Dime Box. Such a terrible tragedy. But what on earth is Nick doing..."

"...Nicholson Rafland." A third voice. "My dear, you don't know the family? You should *hear* the stories. Back at the turn of the century they had an enormous old ranch out east of here, and people say Nick's absolutely obsessed with buying back all the land his father and his grandfather sold off when they..."

The man ignored the whispers and walked into the room. There were sharply etched bones under his tanned skin, and his dark eyes had a distinctive, faintly oblique setting. Intelligent eyes. Angry eyes. Relentless eyes. A startlingly sensual mouth, disciplined to reticence. Laura felt a curious little frisson of premonition.

"Yes?" she said. It was ridiculously inadequate, of course, but apparently no one else in the room was going to say anything to him. "Are you looking for someone?"

"I'm looking for you," he said. His voice was slow and deep, a voice that might have been pleasant if it hadn't been so inexplicably caustic. "The charming and delightful Miss Finesse. The *Times-Capital*'s celebrated life-style columnist. Mistress of the finer points of etiquette and entertaining and decorating and gracious living in general. So we meet at last."

Laura took a deep breath and stared back at him with every atom of self-assurance she could muster. It wasn't easy, because the real Laura, not the lady on the outside but Laura-on-the-inside, was understandably flustered and uncertain in the face of his abrupt appearance and his unaccountable hostility.

"So we do," she said, in the lady's cool civil I-can-cope-with-anything voice. "It's quite obvious that you already know who I am. Perhaps you'd care to introduce yourself."

"My name is Rafland," the dark man said. "But then you don't really have to ask me that, do you, Miss Finesse? You have a better reason than most people to know a Rafland when you see one. To know me when you see me."

"I don't know what you're talking about," Laura said. "I recognize your name, Mr. Rafland, but I assure you that I don't have any particular reason to know you when I see you. Now, you're interrupting my presentation. If you want to talk to me about something, perhaps you could call my office at the paper and make an appointment."

Something flickered briefly in his eyes, behind the anger and the relentlessness. It might almost have been admiration. And it was definitely surprise. For some mysterious reason, she had surprised him.

"You've got courage, at least," he said softly. "When your back's to the wall. Oh, I'm perfectly well aware of the fact that I'm interrupting you, Miss Finesse. I have a very good reason for interrupting you."

He started to walk toward her. Laura watched him come closer, frozen in place with nothing but a silver spoon in her hand. When he was a step or two away from the podium he raised his right hand and reached quite casually inside the front of his jacket.

Laura clutched the spoon. The silver felt suddenly cold.

He took out a plain white business envelope, thick with folded papers.

"Feeling a little anxious?" he said. There was a mocking edge to his voice. "A little apprehensive? The effect of a guilty conscience, perhaps."

"How *dare* you?" Laura said. Her heart was pounding. "I don't have a guilty conscience. I haven't done anything to feel guilty about. What is it that you *want* from me, Mr. Rafland?"

He put the envelope on the podium in front of her. Without thinking she looked down at it, looked at his hand. Inconsequent details jumped out at her: the strong symmetrical bone structure of his wrist and fingers. A narrow line of white shirt cuff showing at the edge of his dark gray jacket sleeve. Square gold cuff links engraved with a symbol she had never seen before, a deeply incised solid circle eclipsing all but a narrow crescent of a bright circle behind it. She frowned and looked up at him again.

"Kit is dead," he said softly, with such slow focused ferocity that each separate word seemed to flash briefly in the air between them. "In a stupid pointless highway accident, three months ago. Or don't you read your own newspaper? My brother is dead. The man who was your husband is dead. Has it occurred to you for one single moment in these past three months to wonder what's happened to your two little girls?"

"My two little girls?" Laura said, in blank bewilderment. "I don't have two little girls."

"You've certainly spent the last six years acting as if you don't," Nicholson Rafland said bitterly. "But for whatever it may be worth to you, Miss Finesse, Emily and Becky are safe. They're with me. And they're going to stay with me."

Laura stared at him, stunned into speechlessness.

"Kit didn't leave a will," he said. "He didn't leave any papers at all. That's why I've had the adoption agreement in that envelope drawn up. Read it. Show it to your lawyer, if you have one. Sign it. You'll need a notary and two witnesses."

"I have never been married," Laura said distinctly. "Not to your brother. Not to anyone. I have no children. Mr. Rafland, you're making a serious mistake."

"Ah, yes," he said contemptuously. "Of course. I suppose that even in today's indiscriminate world you have to make some sort of an effort to protect your public image. Miss Finesse, the perfect lady. The lady who writes such crisp and clever and exceedingly refined advice on etiquette and gracious living. You can hardly admit that you were heartless and selfish and... Shall we say ungracious? Ungracious enough to abandon a year-old child and an infant. Ungracious enough to live in the same city with them for six years and never make so much as a telephone call."

"You're making a *mistake,*" Laura said again.

"Kit was the one who made the mistake," Nicholson Rafland said. A momentary huskiness stirred under the tightly controlled surface of his voice and was gone. "And he suffered for it. Emmie and Becky suffered for it, too. But I'm going to take care of them now. I'm going to make them safe and happy. And secure. For the first time in their lives, secure."

"You don't—" Laura began.

"Just sign the papers," he said. "And return them to my office by the end of next week. Or as God is my witness, I *promise* you. I will make you very, very sorry."

He turned, and seemed to see the other women in the room for the first time. "Ladies," he said courteously, with the faintest sketch of a gesture that might have been a touch of a hat brim, if he'd been wearing a hat. And then without another word he walked out of the room and shut the door behind him.

Laura was furious.

The divided highway ended at Elgin. The rest of the road to Old Dime Box was ordinary four-lane asphalt, weathered and gray. *On the highway between Austin and Dime Box,* one of the Austin League ladies had whispered. *Such a terrible tragedy...* The tragedy had been the death of Nicholson Rafland's brother Christopher in a fiery head-on auto crash.

Oh, the Austin League ladies had been more than happy to tell her all about Kit Rafland and his heedless self-centered young wife. Ex-wife. Sharon Scott. She had been the original Miss Finesse, although it had been almost a year since she'd left the paper, left Austin, full of flamboyant self-congratulation about a new job and a new lover in California.

There had never been a personal byline on the Miss Finesse column. Instead of a photo there was a pen-and-ink sketch of a smug-looking Victorian lady in a lace collar. Sharon Scott and her former husband had been completely, bitterly estranged. And so apparently Kit Rafland had never known she was gone.

Obviously Kit's family never knew it, either.

I'm not going to wait until Monday, Laura fumed as she drove. I don't care if it is seven o'clock on a Friday evening. I don't care if I did have to cancel my appointment with the man from the antique shop who wants to look at some of Aunt Grace's furniture. We'll just see how Nicholson Rafland likes being surprised. We'll see how he likes being *interrupted.*

Two little girls. Two little motherless fatherless girls.

That was the real heart of it all.

Laura's fingers tightened on the steering wheel. I know what it feels like to be motherless, she thought. Motherless and fatherless, brotherless and sisterless. Husbandless and childless. All alone. The last of the Gardiners, as Aunt Grace used to say. Although not even that, not really, not by blood. Only by adoption. She never even let me call her *Mother...*

And now that she's gone I'm not part of any family anymore. Not part of anything.

Oh, God, what I wouldn't give for two little girls of my own. I'm almost tempted, almost tempted, to let him go on believing that I am Sharon Scott. How can he not know that I'm a different person? And if he doesn't know, then why should I enlighten him?

She almost missed the narrow red dirt turnoff. *It's the first crossroad after Dime Box,* one of the Austin League ladies had said. *That all used to be Black Moon land out there along Yegua Creek.* Through her teeth Laura murmured something surprisingly unladylike, something she never would have dreamed of saying if there had been anyone to hear her. Then she threw the little red Probe into reverse and took the turn.

The April dusk was gathering, and warm golden light in tall windows defined the shape of the house. It was two-storied, square and airy, with a plank-and-post veranda all around. Laura skidded to a stop and flung out of the Probe with a deliberate challenging slam of its door. Only then did she realize that there were three people sitting on the veranda in the shadowy twilight.

Nicholson Rafland stood up slowly. He was wearing faded jeans and an open-necked green denim shirt, and without the conventional civilizing effect of a suit and a tie to temper him he seemed more darkly and formidably powerful than ever. The two children stood up, too, silent and wide-eyed, pressing against him on either side. His hands skimmed very softly, very protectively, over the curves of their fragile silky heads. The smaller one, the younger one, wrapped her arms around his leg with utter and artless confidence.

Laura stopped halfway around the car, staring at them, the two children and the tall man with his unexpectedly gentle hands. The kinship, the affinity, were as vivid and unmistakable as a circle of light around them. I've never known what love like that feels like, she thought suddenly, her anger evaporating, the hunger in her heart poignant as the edge of a knife. He's their family and they're his family....

"Why, Miss Finesse," Nicholson Rafland said, breaking the spell. "I should have known that you'd be anxious to divest yourself of your...responsibilities, once and for all. Give me the papers, then, and go. You're not welcome on Black Moon land."

Laura saw the change in the little girls' faces at the sound of the sobriquet. She frowned and took a step forward. "Don't," she said. "Don't call me that, Mr. Rafland, not in front of them. Don't you understand that—"

"Uncle Nick," the older girl interrupted anxiously. "Is that the *real* Miss Finesse? Really truly?"

"Miss *Finesse,*" the little girl said. "Oh. *Oh.*"

She broke away from her sister and her uncle and ran down the steps.

Without stopping to think Laura crouched down in the dust of the driveway and opened her arms. The child had a wiry little tomboy's body, and she caught at Laura's neck with surprising strength, half choking, half crying.

"We knew you'd c-c-come," she sobbed. "Me and Emily. We talked about it, just the two of us, over and over. We knew you'd come back, even though Daddy always said you wouldn't. And then Daddy got k-k-k... He got k..." She couldn't say the word. She burrowed her face into Laura's shoulder and cried harder. Laura bent her own head, her throat tight.

"Uncle Nick?" Emily Rafland's tremulous voice insisted. "Is it?"

"For what little it's worth," Laura heard Nick Rafland say, with bitter irony. "Yes, Emmie, that's the real Miss Finesse."

Laura looked up. Over Becky's dark head she met his eyes. This, of course, was the moment to speak. This was the moment to tell him. This was the moment to tell Becky, too, and Emily standing there with her eyes the size of saucers, that although she was the real Miss Finesse she wasn't the first Miss Finesse, and that the mother they'd never known hadn't come home after all.

"Miss Finesse?" Becky whispered, against her ear. "Will you stay now, with me and Emily? Me and Emily and Uncle Nick?"

"Oh, Becky," Laura said. Her eyes stung. "You don't understand. I can't—"

Becky's arms tightened. There was desperation in the feel of it. "Yes, you can," she said. "Promise. Promise, cross your heart and hope to die. You won't ever go away, not ever anymore."

Laura felt a single treacherous tear spill over and slip down her cheek. She shook it away, hugged Becky one last time and stood up. Her knees were a little unsteady. She walked to the car and opened the door and took her purse from the passenger seat. Then she walked back around the car and up the steps and across the veranda to where Nick Rafland was standing.

Her hands shook as she opened the flap of the purse and took out her wallet. She wrenched the wallet open to the little plastic window where she carried her driver's license and threw it down on the old wicker table in front of him.

He frowned. He picked up the wallet and looked at it, looked at the name and the picture on the license. Then he looked up at her again.

"Gardiner," he said blankly. "Laura Lavinia Gardiner. But that isn't right."

She took the white envelope out of her purse and dropped it on the table as well. "It is right," she said. "You're the one who's wrong."

"Miss Finesse?"

Becky had followed her back onto the veranda. She looked up, with huge dark eyes that were exactly the same distinctive shape and color as Nick Rafland's own. Her hand crept trustfully into Laura's own. "Miss Finesse?" she said again. "I'm going to be a daffodil in a play at my school next Tuesday night. The Melrose Hall School, in Austin. Will you come and see me? Will you?"

"I'm in it, too," Emily piped up shyly. "I have a part with words to say. A poem. All by myself. All the mothers and fathers..." Her voice faltered, and she swallowed hard. "All the grown-ups," she corrected herself, "are going to be there."

Laura hesitated. Nick Rafland stood as if he had been turned to stone, holding the open wallet.

After what seemed like forever he put the wallet down on the table. "Would you please wait here for a few minutes,

Miss Gardiner?" he said abruptly. "Emmie. Becky. It's dark. It's time for you to go inside."

"No," Becky said mutinously. "I want to stay up. I want to stay up all night. Don't you, too, Emily?"

"Yes," Emily whispered.

Nick Rafland looked down at them, and all of a sudden he smiled. It changed his face completely and unexpectedly. He was not entirely inflexible, then, not entirely harsh and hostile. He could be warm. He could be responsive. He could be surprisingly tender....

"I doubt that Miss Finesse wants to stay up all night," he said gently. "And anyway, I need to talk to her myself. Boring grown-up talk." He picked Becky up and took Emily's hand. "Come on. Inside. Baths and bed."

"But I want to stay up," Becky persisted. There was a frightened little quaver in her voice. "If I go to bed, Miss Finesse might not be here in the m-morning. And I want her to come to the *p-p-play.*"

It was impossible not to respond to that. Laura took half a step forward. "It's all right, Becky," she said. "You can go in. Listen, honey. You're right about tomorrow morning. I won't be able to be here. But I'll come to your play next week. I promise I will. Cross my heart and hope to die."

For just a moment Nick Rafland looked at her. He had stopped smiling. Laura looked back at him defiantly.

"And I always..." she said, "always...*always* keep my promises."

He was gone much longer than just a few minutes. Apparently he was putting Emily and Becky to bed himself, and not just handing them over to a flotilla of waiting housekeepers and nannies. Laura flung herself down in one of the comfortable old wicker chairs, watched the quarter-moon rise in the west and tried to make sense of it all.

Miss Finesse? Will you stay now, with me and Emily?

How, she thought, how, how could those two wonderful little girls know their own mother by nothing but a lifeless, meaningless newspaper pseudonym?

And how could Nick Rafland, quite clearly nobody's fool, look straight at me, Laura Gardiner, straight at my face, and still believe that I was his brother's former wife?

Dark as they were, his eyes weren't really black. They weren't blue or gray or any of the cool colors. They were brown. And when he smiled there was a hint of something warm, something vital, something almost coppery in the depths of their darkness.

"Miss Gardiner?"

She looked up. He was standing in the doorway, and from his thoughtful expression he had been watching her silently for some time before he spoke. Laura frowned and shook back her hair.

"I'm still here," she said tartly.

He walked over to the table. "I'm sorry," he said. "If I'd realized that getting Emmie and Becky settled down was going to take so long, I would have asked you to come into the house instead of leaving you to sit on the porch like this."

"It doesn't matter," Laura said. "You did say that you wanted to talk to me?"

"Yes," he said. He didn't sit down. "Where is she?"

"I don't know," Laura said. There was no need to ask him who he meant. "She was already gone when I took over the Miss Finesse column, and I never knew her personally. The women at the Austin League said she'd moved to California."

"When?"

"I don't *know,*" Laura said again. "Not quite a year ago. There was some man."

"There always was."

Laura frowned. "I think you should forget about Sharon Scott for a few minutes," she said. "We need to talk about what you and I are going to do, here and now."

He took a breath. "Of course," he said. "Although I hardly know where to begin. Any kind of an apology seems . . . so completely inadequate."

"I don't care about an apology. That's not what I mean."

"Still," he said. "I am sorry. I'm very sorry. And I'll do whatever I can to make it right. I'll call the president of the Austin League on Monday morning. I'll tell her that what I said to you this afternoon was . . . a mistake."

"What you said in front of Emily and Becky just now," Laura said sharply, "was an even bigger mistake."

He hesitated again. "You mean," he said at last, "that I called you Miss Finesse."

"Yes," Laura said.

You called me Miss Finesse, she thought, and Becky ran down the steps to me. Oh, God, it felt so good when she wrapped her arms around my neck and held on to me so tightly. It felt so good when she came up beside me and slipped her hand into mine and said *I'm going to be a daffodil in a play at my school next week. . . .*

"I called you Miss Finesse," he said again, more slowly. "And even though I've just spent half an hour trying to explain, I don't think I really convinced them that you're not . . . not the other Miss Finesse. All right. I made a mistake. What do you think I should do about it?"

"I think you should sit down," Laura said, "and explain how all of this could have happened in the first place."

He didn't move at first. Then with one abrupt decisive gesture he pulled out a chair and sat down. "If you want an explanation," he said, "I suppose I owe you an explanation. Where would you like me to start?"

"Start," Laura said, "with why you didn't know as soon as you saw me that I wasn't Sharon Scott."

"I never met her," Nick Rafland said. "She wanted Kit all to herself, and so of course she didn't want anything to do with a family like the Raflands. Especially with me."

"I don't understand."

"My family," Nick said dryly, "can be overwhelming. There are so many of us. And Kit and I were twins. Identical twins."

"I wondered," Laura said, "why the girls looked so much like you. Becky, especially. Enough to be your own."

"In a way I feel as if they are my own," he said. "Kit and I were the same… Well, we were always very close. Until he met Sharon Scott. Do you have brothers and sisters, Miss Gardiner?"

"Laura," she said. "Please don't call me Miss Gardiner."

It makes me sound like Aunt Grace, she thought. Who wasn't my aunt at all, of course. What does it feel like, I wonder, to grow up being part of a family, a family so big it's overwhelming?

"No," she said aloud. "I don't have any brothers and sisters."

She thought she had kept all the emotion out of her voice. But Nick Rafland leaned forward just a bit and looked at her curiously, almost as if he could see past her carefully nurtured poised-and-ladylike facade.

That, of course, was impossible. No one had ever seen past it. Not Aunt Grace. Not even Jeff. Still, it was an oddly intimate gesture, that little shift of his weight in the chair, that barely perceptible heightening of the concentration in his dark eyes, almost as intimate as if he had reached out and touched her physically. Suddenly, involuntarily, Laura shivered.

"I have nine of them," he said quietly, as if nothing out of the ordinary had happened. "I'm sorry. Eight. Five sisters and…three brothers. Are you cold? Would you like to go inside?"

"No," Laura said brusquely. "I suppose I can understand why you didn't know me by sight, then, if you never met your sister-in-law. But surely you knew her name."

"I knew hers, of course," he said. "I didn't know yours."

"How could you not know my name? You must have called the paper this afternoon to find out where I was."

He shrugged. "I did," he said. "But I just asked them for Miss Finesse. That was all Kit ever called her, you see, after she left him. All any of us in the family ever called her. Even Emmie and Becky. We called her Miss Finesse." He said it with a surprising amount of bitterness and sarcasm.

"It doesn't sound as if you meant it as much of a compliment," Laura said slowly.

"We didn't. The whole thing was...ironic, to say the least. She abandoned her husband and her two babies, all without so much as a backward glance. And yet in public she was Miss Finesse. The ultimate authority on manners and morals and gracious living."

"But Becky didn't say it like that," Laura said. "Becky was glad to see...to see Miss Finesse. She said she and Emily had been waiting for her to come back."

"Becky's six years old," Nick Rafland said. "She doesn't understand. She and Emmie have had...an unsettled life. The Miss Finesse they've been waiting for is a lonely little girls' fantasy. She doesn't exist. She isn't coming back."

"You're the one who doesn't understand," Laura said. The words seemed to be saying themselves, without any conscious volition on her part. "She does exist. And she has come back."

Silence.

He looked at her for a moment, and then he leaned back in his chair. "Has she now," he said softly. "I suppose you mean yourself."

"Is that so impossible?" Laura demanded. "Listen, Mr. Rafland. Nick. I didn't start this. You did. But I'm willing to follow it through. I *want* to follow it through."

"You can't seriously think," he said, "that I would allow Emmie and Becky to go on believing that you're their mother."

"No," Laura said. Her voice wavered just a little. "Of course not. Not their real mother."

"And not some kind of a make-believe mother figure, either," Nick Rafland said. His voice, too, was not quite as steady as it had been. "They have to know the truth. That I made a mistake. That there's more than one Miss Finesse. And that you won't be able to come to the play next week, after all."

"Oh, no," Laura said. "No. I'm not going to let you do that to me. I *promised.*"

Nick Rafland stood up. "I'm sure you mean well," he said. "But if you come to the play, it will only encourage Emmie and Becky to attach themselves to you. More than they already have."

"I understand that," Laura began. "But I—"

"Wait," he said. "Let me finish. They've lost their father. They never knew their mother. They're so vulnerable right now. I don't want them to lose anyone else they care about. And eventually you'll stop making your promises. You'll get tired of them and go back to your own life."

Laura came to her feet as well. "I won't," she said. "And I'm coming to the play. I promised them I would."

"Don't. I don't want you to. I'll explain to Emmie and Becky about the promise."

The moonlight only emphasized the tense muscles at the corner of his jaw, the hard purposeful line of his mouth. His hair was so black that it absorbed the light completely, like the pelt of a night-hunting cat. And yet with the two little girls, he had smiled. His face had changed. He had been so warm and so responsive and so instinctively, profoundly gentle. . . .

"Melrose Hall School," Laura said stubbornly. "Next Tuesday night. Becky's going to be a daffodil."

"No," Nick Rafland said.

Laura's hands were icy, and she could feel her own heart beating. Again she saw Becky's dark beseeching eyes turned up to hers, heard Emily's soft shy hesitant voice. *All the grown-ups*. . . She lifted her chin.

"Yes," she said.

Chapter Two

Nick had just introduced himself to Emmie's English teacher when the tall slender woman with the straight shining ash brown hair walked through the door to the Melrose Hall School auditorium as if she had every right in the world to be there.

"Uncle Nick!" Becky, in her ruffled yellow daffodil dress, caught at his sleeve. "Oh, Uncle Nick, look! It's Miss Finesse. You were wrong. She did come, just like she promised."

"So she did," Nick said. The delight in Becky's voice surprised him a little. She and Emmie had eventually accepted his explanations, his reassurances, so calmly. All the while had they been so anxious to see Laura Gardiner again? He frowned. "Well, since she's here," he said, "why don't you and Emmie—"

Too late. Becky was already running across the room with her daffodil flounces flying. The English teacher smiled, murmured a platitude, and moved away. Emmie took a step closer to him and slipped her hand into his.

"I know you said she's not really our...not the *real* Miss Finesse," she said, in her soft serious voice. "But she did keep her promise. She came to the play. And she's nice, isn't she? Don't you think she's nice?"

Laura Gardiner had leaned down to say something to Becky, who was tugging on her skirt, wrinkling the crisp pale gray linen. Laura didn't seem to mind. She laughed. Her face, which was just a trifle too determined and strong-chinned to be called an oval, flushed suddenly, as if it had been lit from within.

"Don't you?" Emmie persisted, tugging on his hand.

Nick looked down. Sweet earnest Emmie, he thought, so conscious of being the older sister, grave and shy and stubborn as a baby bulldog when she had a question she wanted an answer to. She was dressed as a rain shower, in gray tights and a leotard sewn with fringes of silver tinsel. "Yes," he said, a little unwillingly. Only when he heard himself saying it did he realize that it was actually true. "Yes, Emmie, I think she's nice."

Becky came dancing up, holding Laura Gardiner by the hand. "Miss Finesse says I look bee-yoo-tiful," she crowed. "She says I look ex . . . ex . . . ex-something."

"Exemplary," Laura Gardiner said. She shook back her hair and looked at him with a curious combination of entreaty and defiance. Her eyes were transparent crystal gray with the very faintest, most intriguing suggestion of violet. "The perfect daffodil, don't you think? And Emily. Hi, honey. Now, I wonder if I can guess what you're going to be. Hold out your arms and let me see."

Emmie colored up with inarticulate pleasure and waved her arms. The strips of tinsel fluttered.

"Rain," Laura said. "Of course. It's April, and you're an April shower. Am I right?"

"Yes," Emmie whispered. "And I have a poem to say, too."

"I remember," Laura said. "Did you have to spend a long time learning it?"

"Pretty long. But I can say it without one single mistake. Can't I, Uncle Nick?"

"You certainly can," Nick said. "And so can I, for that matter. Well, Miss Gardiner. Laura. Here you are, despite what I said to you on Friday night."

She had an odd contradictory way of lowering her head so that the curve of her hair swung forward to veil her profile, standing very still for a moment, and then looking up unexpectedly, shaking the silky fall back with quick candid impatience. "Here I am," she acknowledged. "I did promise."

"Apparently I was wrong again," he said slowly. "The girls would have been crushed, I think, if you hadn't been here."

"Uncle Nick told us that you probably wouldn't come," Becky confided guilelessly. "So we wouldn't get our feelings hurt, he said. But we knew you would, me and Emily. And you're going to come and get ice cream with us, too, after the play, aren't you?"

"Miss Gardiner may have other plans for the rest of the evening," Nick said.

"That sounds wonderful," Laura said, at the same time. "I'd love to."

They both hesitated for a moment. Then he said, "I'm sorry."

"I'm sorry," she said, exactly simultaneously.

Again they both hesitated, each unwilling to be the first to speak next, each waiting for the other.

And then all of a sudden she laughed, just as she'd laughed when Becky ran up to her and crumpled her skirt. For the briefest of instants the poised and impeccable lady vanished and she was a different person, luminous and lighthearted. Nick stared at her, a little stunned.

"Emily. Rebecca. It's time to get ready." A harassed-looking blond woman in a blue and white print dress had come up behind them. "Run along backstage, now, and find your places. You've been wonderful with those girls,

Mr. Rafland," she added, as she watched Emmie and Becky thread their way through the crowd to the door beside the stage. "Under such very difficult circumstances for all of you." She turned to Laura Gardiner and grinned ruefully. "They made me the stage manager this year and I had no idea it would be so much work. I'm Kathy Lane, Melinda's mother. You must be Mrs. Rafland."

It was the last thing Nick was expecting. And yet it plucked at something, something that he didn't know he'd been thinking, a forgotten dream perhaps, or an impulse come and gone too quickly to be a conscious image. *You must be Mrs. Rafland....*

This tall slender mystifyingly tenacious woman, this stranger, this Laura Gardiner, what would she be like, there, always there, at the ranch, at the house in town? What would she be like at the breakfast table, at the dinner table, working, playing, making ordinary everyday conversation? What would she be like at night, in the darkness, that spill of shimmering light brown hair spread out over his pillow, her head thrown back and her smooth pale throat...

"How do you do," Laura Gardiner said pleasantly, a lady again, courteous and composed and equal to anything. "Actually my name is Laura Gardiner. I'm a...friend of the family, that's all. Emily and Becky told me about the play and Nick was generous enough to invite me to see it."

There was a trace of the South in her voice. Not Texas. The deep South. It was elusive and velvety and for all her self-possessed ladylike elegance, surprisingly provocative. Contradictory. As so many things about Laura Gardiner seemed to be contradictory.

I have never been married, she had said, Friday afternoon at the Driskill. *I have no children.* He had made it his business to find out if she had been telling the truth. She had. Yet it was easy to see that she loved children. And from the way Emmie and Becky had responded to her, she was obviously one of those rare adults that children themselves loved and trusted on sight.

Why, then? Why no husband? Why no family of her own?

"...together, don't you think, Mr. Rafland?"

He came back to himself with a start. Kathy Lane and Laura Gardiner were looking at him expectantly. He had no idea at all of what Mrs. Lane had asked him.

She laughed. "Good heavens, you look as if you were a million miles away," she said. "The play is about to start, and I was simply suggesting that you and Miss Gardiner find a place. The seats are filling up, and of course you'll want to sit together."

"Together," Nick repeated. "Oh. Yes. Of course. We'll want to sit together."

"You dealt with that remarkably well," Nick Rafland said.

Laura was sitting next to him at the end of the second row. There was only one armrest for the two of them to share. Laura's own forearm in its tailored gray linen jacket sleeve rested lightly against one side of it. Nick kept his arm close to his body.

He was wearing the gold cuff links again, with the dark circle superimposed on the light. He must wear them all the time, Laura thought. That strange symbol must mean something to him.

"Dealt with what?" she said.

"Mrs. Lane's assumption that you were..." He hesitated. His oblique dark eyes were thoughtful, and he wasn't a man who made it easy to guess exactly what it was that he was thinking. "That you were my wife," he went on at last.

"It wasn't such an unreasonable guess," Laura said. "We were standing there together, after all, with the children. What did you expect me to do, scream and faint?"

He smiled for the first time that evening. He really did have a remarkable mouth, full and clear-cut and sensitive and at the same time self-contained, inscrutable. His teeth were very white against his tanned skin. "Nothing quite that dramatic," he said. "But you might have been just a bit more disconcerted at the thought. I have to admit that I was."

"I can't imagine why," she said.

He looked at her quizzically. Then very deliberately he shifted his arm two or three inches so that it lay casually on the armrest next to hers. Through her own silk and linen, through his dark blue wool and white broadcloth, impossible as it was, for a moment Laura thought she could feel the living warmth of his skin. Involuntarily she pulled her arm away.

"Oh, I think you can," he murmured.

"I don't know what you're talking about," Laura said.

Yes, you do, Laura-on-the-inside whispered. Where on earth did that feeling come from, that sudden sensitivity, that moment when you couldn't quite catch your breath? You've never felt anything like that before. Even with Jeff you never felt it. If you'd been able to feel it then, all those years ago, things might have been so very, very different....

She smoothed studiously at the creases in her skirt, as if that were her only reason for moving her arm. "I am surprised, though, that a man like you isn't married," she said, after a moment. "That you don't have a real wife."

He looked away. For a second or two he didn't seem to be in the auditorium at all. Regret and self-mockery and something that might once have been passion flickered in the shape of his mouth. Then it was gone. He looked at her again and smiled.

"The last thing I want," he said mildly, "is a real wife. Or a make-believe wife, for that matter. But since you bring it up, I'm surprised, too. You obviously love children. But you don't seem to have a real husband. A real family of your own."

"No," Laura said. "I don't."

"But don't you ever want—" he began.

"No," she said again.

Another man would probably have asked more questions. Nick Rafland did nothing but look at her with that dark enigmatic thoughtfulness in his eyes.

"You're thinking something," Laura said uneasily. "What?"

"That you and I have more in common than I realized," he said. "A great deal more, in fact."

"Just because neither one of us wants to get married?"

"There's that," he said. "There's the way you seem to feel about Emmie and Becky, of course, and the way they obviously feel about you. There are one or two other things that you don't know I know about you. And there's this, of course."

She had her hands folded neatly in her lap. Without making any particular fuss about it he reached over and actually touched her wrist, brushed the backs of his loosely curled fingers very lightly and quickly across her skin. Laura drew in her breath.

"Don't do that," she said sharply. "I don't like it."

He had already taken his hand away. "Don't you?" he murmured. "I'm sorry."

"And what do you mean, you know one or two other things that I don't know you know about me?"

He shrugged very slightly. "I was curious," he said. "That's all. I wasn't sure if you'd be here tonight or not, but if there was even a chance that you were going to have anything to do with Emmie and Becky I wanted to know more about you. I asked a couple of my researchers to—"

A sudden clamor of recorded music overrode his voice. There was a flurry at the back of the room, and the level was hastily adjusted. Then the curtain began to rise.

"Perfect timing," Laura said. "But if you think I'm not going to keep asking you about what your researchers found out and why you thought you had any right to be doing research on me in the first place, you're wrong."

He smiled. Dark and self-possessed and formidable as he was, he did have an extraordinarily appealing smile. "What, again?" he said.

"Oh, yes," Laura said. "Again."

"I think I'm going to write a column," Laura said, "about the etiquette of eating ice cream cones."

Becky leaned across the round wrought-iron table, her dark eyes shining. Laura snatched up a napkin and caught the scoop of bright pink peppermint stick ice cream just as it started to topple off her cone. Becky frowned, patted the top of the ice cream firmly with one palm as if to say *You stay there, now,* and then took an enormous openmouthed lick. "What's etty...etty...etty-whatever-it-was?" she demanded.

"Etiquette," Laura repeated, with a smile. "It's kind of another way of saying 'finesse.' Courtesy. Good manners."

"Eating peppermint ice cream without spreading it from one end of the table to the other," Nick Rafland suggested.

He had taken off his jacket and tie and pulled the curiously engraved gold links out of his shirt cuffs so that he could fold them back. The clean starched broadcloth looked vividly white against the sun-browned skin on the inner surface of his wrists and the crisp, vigorous dark hair on the hard outer curve of his forearms. He was eating a single scoop of bittersweet chocolate-coffee ice cream, very neatly, from a cup, not a cone.

"It's all right, Uncle Nick," Becky said, stroking him lovingly on the arm and leaving a smear of peppermint pink on his immaculate shirtsleeve. "Miss Finesse has lots of napkins."

"And a good thing, too," he said mildly. "Eat it, sweetheart, don't play with it. Laura?"

He held out his hand. She gave him one of the napkins. Their fingers touched briefly.

"Thank you," he said. "Mom."

"I'm just trying to be helpful," Laura said a little defensively. "And I don't think you should call me that, Nick, even as a joke. You're the one who said you didn't want the girls to see me as a make-believe—" She stopped. Emily and Becky were watching her, bright-eyed as two squirrels. "You know," she said. "Anyway, I'm not a 'mom' type."

"Really? And what is a 'mom' type?"

"I can type," Becky interpolated proudly. "I'm learning at school, on the computer."

Nick laughed and began to dab at the patch of ice cream on his sleeve. It was all so natural and so casual that for a moment it seemed as if they had been together forever, as if they were a real family, sitting there in the tiny brightly lighted green-and-white ice cream shop with the soft spring darkness pressing in at the windows all around them. Laura's throat tightened. She looked down and took a small polite bite of her own vanilla-pecan-praline.

"Et-i-quette," Emily said seriously, as if she were memorizing the word for a school spelling test. Her own cone of natural-juice orange sherbet was beginning to drip a little. "We like to come here a lot, Miss Gardiner, so maybe you should explain to us about the et-i-quette of eating ice cream cones."

Laura passed another napkin across the table. "It's really pretty simple," she said. "Look. The idea is to get the ice cream down inside the cone so it won't drip, and so you can eat the cone itself. You start out by licking around the edges like this."

She demonstrated. Against her tongue the vanilla ice cream was smooth and chaste and cold, nubbled with hidden bits of pecan and chewy-crisp brown sugar candy. Emily and Becky watched her and copied her exactly.

"Then you lick the top and press the ice cream down at the same time," Laura went on. "Very, very carefully, now. You don't want to break the cones."

"Your lingual dexterity," Nick Rafland murmured, "is a fascinating thing to watch."

"You didn't even have the fortitude to get a cone," Laura retorted under her breath. "So don't sit there and talk to me about lingual dexterity." She turned back to the two little girls. "Then you lick all the way around again," she said, "and press down again, and keep doing it until all the ice cream's inside the cone. See?"

"I can do it," Becky said triumphantly. "Look, Emily. Look, Uncle Nick."

She and Emily compared their cones, one bright candy pink, one creamy pale orange. As different as they themselves are, Laura thought. There's an idea. I wonder what everyone would say if I turned in a column about how the choice of a flavor in an ice cream shop can reveal a person's character?

Emily, now, only seven but so grave and serious and shy, picked natural-juice orange sherbet. Not a typical child's choice. Some substance, some tartness with the sweetness. On the other hand, exuberant little six-year-old Becky wanted peppermint stick, bright pink and filled with chips of spicy-sweet red-and-white candy. Exactly like her. Exactly right.

Nick Rafland's dark head was bent toward his nieces, inspecting their cone-etiquette prowess. His own ice cream was only half eaten. Dark, dark bittersweet chocolate-coffee. A subtle and complex flavor, Laura thought, with no nuts or chips or other nonessentials to detract from its concentrated sensory impact. And in a cup, not a cone, eaten slowly, with such cool deliberate fully adult precision.

And what about you, Miss Laura Lavinia? she asked herself. Apply your unique new theory of ice-cream-cone-psychoanalysis to yourself. You're a bland pristine plain-vanilla lady, with all your bits of pecan and praline, all your peculiarities, all the things you love and all the things you feel and all the things you want, carefully hidden away. Yes, that's you. Cold and uninteresting. Just what Jeff called you, over and over again...

"She will so, *too,*" Becky said. Out of nowhere she sounded close to tears. "She came to the play, didn't she? She *will.*"

Laura blinked. "I will what?" she said.

"Nothing," Nick said. All of a sudden he sounded brusque and a little tired.

"It *is* something," Emily whispered.

"Emmie," he said gently. Emily gulped and swallowed her words and leaned closer to him, clutching his wrist. Becky stared at Laura wordlessly, a plea in her eyes. The orange cone and the pink cone lay on the table, melting, forgotten.

"You might as well let them tell me," Laura said.

Nick took a breath. "All right," he said. "Becky?"

"You're Miss *Finesse,*" Becky said passionately. "Even though you're not that other Miss Finesse. You can teach us etty...etty-kett things and so now we have a fem...a fem...a fem-something like Aunt Linda says we should have and we want you to take us shopping and pick us up after school and do things with us and Uncle Nick says you won't and I think he's *mean.*"

She burst into tears.

Nick stood up. His mouth was grim. "We'd better go home," he said.

"A fem-something?" Laura said.

"A feminine influence," he said. "Something my sisters used to tell Kit that Emmie and Becky needed. Now they've started in on me." He crouched down beside Becky's chair. "Come on, sweetheart," he said. "Don't cry. Here, take the rest of these napkins."

"Don't want to go home if Miss Finesse isn't coming," Becky sobbed. "Want us all to stay here together."

"Shh," Nick said. "Do you know what? Miss Gardiner is going to come home with us, just for a little while. Long enough to help me put you to bed."

Laura frowned and opened her mouth to speak. Nick Rafland looked up at her and shook his head once, so quickly and tightly that it was almost unnoticeable.

"Please," he said softly.

"I'm coming," Laura said. She stood up as well and took Emily's hand. Emily leaned against her, trembling, and Laura squeezed her hand reassuringly. "Of course I'm coming. I was just going to ask you if you and I could talk for a while afterward."

"I thought you might say that," he said. "We can talk all night, if you want to."

Nick Rafland's house in town looked out over Lake Travis. His deck, Laura thought, was bigger than the living room in her own tiny renovated Austin-stone cottage in West Lynn. The furniture was nicer, too. Two sides of the deck were screened with lemon trees in tubs, their glossy oval leaves clustering around enormous real lemons. The front of the deck faced northwest, over the lake, and green cliffs dropped away below.

"I thought we were never going to get them to sleep," she said.

Nick had settled himself in a chair on the other side of the deck, one foot in its polished shoe quite casually propped against the railing. "You're very good with them," he said. "They might have known you all their lives."

"A lot of it's the Miss Finesse thing," Laura said. "They really have been waiting for a kind of a magical lady named Miss Finesse to come along and make everything all right for them."

He turned his head and looked at her. "Maybe you were right, last Friday night, out at the ranch," he said. "Maybe she has."

"Maybe," Laura said. "I'd like to think so. But on the other hand, you don't even..." She hesitated. "I was going to say 'you don't even know me,'" she went on. "But you do, don't you? You know all kinds of things about me that I don't know you know."

"Ah," he said. "Yes. The researchers."

"I suppose I'm curious, as much as anything. What on earth did they find out about me?"

"You're from Charleston, South Carolina," he said. "You're thirty-two years old. You were actually born in Sarasota, Florida, although the records there are sealed. When you were two months old you were adopted by a forty-four-year-old woman named Grace Gardiner, who was the last descendent of a very old and very aristocratic Charleston family. She wasn't married. For her to do such a thing was considered a bit... eccentric."

"Oh, yes," Laura said. "It was."

"You always loved horses and won a lot of ribbons in eventing and show jumping when you were a girl. You were presented in the Cotillion Sainte-Anne when you were eighteen. You were engaged to a boy named Jefferson Calhoun for a year or so but he was killed in a riding accident just three days before the wedding." He hesitated. "I'm sorry," he said, in a different voice.

Laura looked out at the lake. All the emotion, the shock and the anguish and the fear, had long since burned away to nothing. Only the sick feeling was left, the sick feeling that rose in her throat whenever a man came close to her. The sick feeling and the endless hopeless guilt...

"It was a long time ago," she said steadily. "Go on."

"You graduated from the University of South Carolina," he said. "You taught English for three years in Charleston. Then Grace Gardiner had a stroke and you took a year off to take care of her. When you were ready to go back to work there weren't any teaching jobs open, so you found a job with a newspaper. Three years ago the two of you came to Austin, and about nine months ago you started writing the Miss Finesse column. Last January Grace Gardiner died, only a few days before Kit was killed."

He stopped. Laura waited, but he said nothing more. Apparently that was all.

"Was it the old and aristocratic Southern family?" she said. It was impossible to keep the very faintest edge of defensiveness out of her voice. "The show jumping? The Cotillion? Just what was it that made you decide that I was a fit person to be associating with Emily and Becky after all?"

He shut his eyes for a moment. Then he looked at her again. "I deserved that, I suppose," he said equably. "I'm sorry. I didn't really have the right to pry into your life, did I?"

"No," Laura said. "You didn't. I'm surprised you didn't find out the titles of the books I borrowed from the library last week. Or just which pieces of Aunt Grace's furniture I have the space to keep and which pieces I'm trying to sell."

He smiled. "The ironic thing," he said, "is that none of it's important anyway. What's important is that you came to the play when you said you would. That you showed the girls the...et-i-quette, as Emmie says, of eating ice cream cones. That you came back here with us tonight, when we needed you."

He was silent for a moment, leaning back in his chair, looking out over the lake. The palm-print of pink peppermint ice cream was still visible on his shirtsleeve. Laura stared at his hand resting on the arm of the chair, at the bony fineness of his fingers and the strong sinewy shape of his wrist. She could see tension in the curve where the muscle of his forearm began. He seemed to be gathering his thoughts, gathering his physical energy itself, for a difficult leap forward.

"Will you come again?" he said at last.

Laura stood up and walked to the edge of the deck. Her heels made sharp tapping noises in the silence. She said, "Last Friday you didn't want me to come."

"I thought we'd agreed that I was wrong about that."

"You already have... How many sisters did you say you have?"

"Five," he said. "And a couple of sisters-in-law."

"Isn't that enough feminine influence for two little girls?"

"They all have different ideas about raising children," he said slowly. "Sometimes the more they try to help, the more confusing things get. And they all have children of their own. I think Emmie and Becky would like to have a... a friend who can provide them with one consistent standard. A friend they can have all to themselves."

Laura took hold of the railing and leaned against it. The scents of spring and the lake and the lemon leaves were everywhere, and the moon was almost too bright and beautiful to be real against the rich dark vastness of the sky. Becky's hand in hers. Emily leaning against her, trembling. Being needed. Being on the inside of the circle. Belonging...

"And you're sure you've changed your mind about the girls becoming attached to a make-believe mother figure?" she said. "A make-believe..." She hesitated for a moment. "A make-believe mom?" she finished, just a little wryly.

"I'm sure," he said. "Someday you're going to have to enlighten me, you know, as to the difference between a mother and a mom."

"Someday," Laura said, "I will. Listen, Nick, I want to do it. I want to very much. But you and I are going to have to be absolutely clear about... about everything."

She heard the chair creak. Nothing else. Was he simply standing there looking at her, or was he walking across the wood of the deck, coming up behind her so quietly that his footsteps made no noise at all? She closed her eyes and held her breath.

His hands touched her shoulders. It was very light but at the same time quite deliberate. "And just what is this everything," he said, "that you want us to be so clear about?"

For a moment she didn't move. For a moment she was no one else but Laura-on-the-inside, and it felt right, all of it, the moon and the lemon leaves and Nick Rafland's touch, more intense and more right than anything else she had ever known. Then time jolted backward and the moment had never happened and she stiffened and stepped away.

"Ah," he said quietly. He made no attempt to follow her, to touch her again. "I see. You really don't like it when I touch you. I thought that it might have been just because we were in the auditorium and there were so many other people around us."

Laura let out her breath and opened her eyes. The scent of the lemon leaves had turned flat and dusty, and the moon looked like nothing but a crumpled white half circle of paper pasted carelessly on a flat black facade. "No," she said steadily. "It wasn't just because we were in the auditorium. I really don't like it when you touch me. I really don't like it when anyone touches me. That's what I want us to be clear about."

"Will you tell me why?"

Aunt Grace's voice, that cool liquid Charleston drawl: *You were born with a hedonistic and disorderly nature, my dear, and you must always struggle against it. Never forget that you are a lady....* Jeff's voice, bitter, contemptuous, on what neither one of them knew was going to be the last night of his life: *You're not normal, Laura, do you know that? You're not even human. No flesh-and-blood woman could ever be as cold as you've been with me, from the very beginning....*

Laura swallowed hard and shook back her hair. "No," she said. "I won't tell you why."

Seconds passed. Minutes. Although she wasn't looking at him Laura could feel the sheer physical power of his height and strength beside her, his concentration, his curiosity, almost but not quite masked by his stillness. At last he said, "All right. I think I'm perfectly clear about...everything. I'd still like you to spend some more time with Emmie and Becky, if you're willing."

Laura took a deep breath. "I'm willing," she said.

"What would you say, then, to a picnic out at the ranch next Saturday? Emmie and Becky and I have been planning to take the day and ride out to look at the wildflowers. Since you ride, too, you might enjoy it. I know they'd love to have you come along."

"I haven't ridden much lately. And I'm not used to western tack."

"I'll give you a very gentle horse."

That was too much. Laura turned to face him. "I was winning ribbons on show jumpers when I was ten," she said tartly. "I can handle any horse you can."

He grinned at her. "So prove it to me."

"All right. I will. What time Saturday?"

"Early. Say seven o'clock?"

"I'll be there."

"We'll be looking forward to it," he said. "All three of us. Emmie. And Becky. And me."

Chapter Three

"Her name is Penny," Nick said. "Penthesilea, actually. The legendary queen of the Amazons."

The legendary queen of the Amazons was a glorious long-legged chestnut mare, neatly tacked up in an English-style endurance saddle and a loose-ring snaffle bridle. Arab blood showed in the shape of her head, the width between her great dark intelligent eyes, the narrow muzzle and flaring sensitive nostrils.

She was so beautiful that it almost hurt to look at her. "Penthesilea," Laura said softly. She held out one hand. "Penny?"

The mare pricked up her ears. Then she lowered her head and laid her muzzle very gently into the hollow of Laura's fingers.

"Penny," Laura whispered again. The mare breathed against her palm. "Oh, Nick, she's wonderful. I had no idea you had horses like this."

"I don't," Nick said. "She's on loan from a breeder friend of mine in San Antonio."

Laura frowned. "On loan since when?" she said.

"Since yesterday afternoon."

"You borrowed her for me?"

He smiled at her, casual and very much at ease in his boots and faded jeans and crisply pressed scarlet cotton shirt. "You said you wanted a show jumper," he said. "My own horses run to working stock and overindulged ponies. If you like her, we'll see about making it permanent."

"Don't be ridiculous," Laura said. "I can't afford a horse like this. And I'm not going to let you buy her just because I might come out here to ride with the girls once in a while."

"There might be some question," Nick said mildly, "as to whether that's entirely up to you. Go ahead, try her."

"It certainly is up to me—" Laura began stiffly.

"Miss Finesse!" Becky called. She was leading her fat chocolate-colored pony out of the barn, dressed like a minuscule feminine version of Nick Rafland himself in boots and jeans and a cotton shirt. With her flyaway dark hair pulled back in a pigtail, the resemblance between the two of them was startling. "I've never seen a saddle like that before. All flat and everything. How are you going to hold on if she starts to buck?"

"I think I can manage to stay on," Laura said. "I took riding lessons for years and years, beginning when I was even younger than you are."

"Oh," Becky said disdainfully. "*Lessons.* We didn't have to take lessons, Emily and me. We just always knew how to ride."

"Always," Emily echoed, following her sister out of the barn. Her pony was white, curried and combed within an inch of its life. "I've seen a saddle like that before, though. In a book, at the library. But you have different clothes on, Miss Gardiner. The lady in the picture had funny pants that stuck out at the sides."

Nick started to laugh. "And Miss Gardiner's pants," he said, "can hardly be said to stick out at the sides. Except in the perfectly delightful places where Miss Gardiner herself—"

"Oh, hush," Laura said. She turned her back on him and said to Emily, "The pants in the picture were probably old-fashioned jodhpurs. Even traditional breeches don't really...well, stick out at the sides very much anymore. What I'm wearing are just called riding tights."

"You should wear jeans to ride," Becky said critically. "And real boots. Not those tall skinny flat-heeled things."

Laura laughed. "Maybe next time I will," she said. "Don't frown at her, Nick, she doesn't mean to be rude. What's your pony's name, honey?"

"Snickers," Becky said. "'Cause he's all brown except he has that kind of light-colored mane and tail like the inside of a Snickers bar. Emily has Pegasus, 'cause he's all white like a picture in a book she read once. She reads books all the time. And Uncle Nick's horse is named Keno."

Keno was an enormous deep-chested bay gelding with a menacing Roman nose. Apparently he didn't much like being tied, because he was standing at the fence shaking his head crossly, the white showing around his eyes. Their picnic lunch was packed in a pair of well-worn pannier baskets. A rifle in a plain scabbard was buckled unobtrusively to the saddle on the near side.

"Now that we've all been introduced," Nick said, "are we ready to go? Laura?"

"I'm ready," Laura said. "At least, I think I'm ready. What on earth are you expecting us to run into out there?"

"Run into?" he repeated. Then he realized that she was looking at the rifle and grinned. "A stray varmint or two, maybe," he said. "There've been rabies cases here in Lee County in the past few years. Would you like a hand up?"

"No, thank you," Laura said. She gathered up the reins, caught the toe of her left boot in the stirrup iron, and vaulted lightly into the saddle. Emily swung onto her placid white pony's back just as easily. Snickers, though, was fractious, sidling away from Becky when she tried to mount.

Nick walked over to the pony and held him while Becky pulled herself up.

"Snickers seems kind of edgy this morning," he said. "Do you think you can manage him?"

"'Course I can," Becky said.

Nick held the pony for just a moment longer. Becky's eyebrows came together mutinously, and she tugged at the reins. "Let go," she said. "I want to ride by myself."

Nick looked at her for a moment, and then he lifted his hand. "All right," he said. "But stay close, sweetheart, and be careful until he's worked off some of that extra energy."

He turned and pulled Keno's reins free of the fence. The girls trotted off down the red dirt driveway. Laura touched Penny lightly with her heels and started after them. Then, for no reason she could have ever explained, she looked back.

A glimpse, like one frame of a film, frozen in time: Keno throwing up his head, switching his tail, sidestepping irritably. Nick's jeaned and booted legs commanding and pliant at once against the big bay gelding's body, the muscles in his arms and shoulders shifting under the glowing scarlet cotton of his shirt, his hands on the reins light and deliberate and skilled. Laura felt a sudden involuntary tremor of sensation, unfamiliar, a little frightening. All the strength in her own legs seemed to be melting and fusing and dissolving away to nothing....

Penny broke stride uncertainly, and Laura clutched at the reins, struggled to regain her balance. When she looked up again Nick was beside her. His dark eyes were curious, mildly concerned. Keno was moving easily, relaxed, under control.

"Are you all right?" Nick said.

"I'm fine," Laura said briefly. She leaned forward, and Penny struck off into an effortless flowing canter. The girls were far ahead, after all. Becky's pony was not entirely to be trusted. And at least one of us, she rationalized to herself, should always be keeping close to them.

* * *

Nick knew, to the moment, to the inch, when they crossed his own property line and stepped onto the land of the old Black Moon.

He knew, too, that the grass and brush weren't really more luxuriant, the new leaves on the trees weren't really greener, the masses of spring bluebonnets weren't really a richer, deeper blue. But they always looked as if they were—heightened, enlarged, intensified by his own hunger to possess the land they grew on.

To possess it again. Because it had been Rafland land once. The burned-out shell of the original ranch house was part of it, the few remaining outbuildings, even the overgrown little family cemetery. It had been Rafland land once, and some day, like all the rest of the Black Moon, it would be Rafland land again.

I will get it back from her, Nick thought grimly. I don't care what it costs....

"You don't care what what costs?"

He looked up sharply. Laura Gardiner was riding beside him, looking as if she'd been born on that elegant chestnut mare. Laura, tall, slight, fragile-looking, but whose slender wrists had to be strong as steel to hold the high-spirited Penny so lightly. The shimmering fall of silk-straight ash brown hair was caught back in a tortoiseshell clip, leaving her profile and the line of her cheek and throat uncharacteristically exposed.

"I didn't realize I'd said that out loud," he said.

"You most certainly did," Laura said. "And you looked as if you meant every word of it. Whatever it is you want so badly, I'm glad I'm not the person you're planning to get it from."

His own transparency irked him, made him want to disconcert her, too. "Oh, but maybe you are," he said.

A very faint flush crept up under her skin. For all that thirty-two-year-old Southern-lady self-assurance, Nick thought suddenly, she blushes like a schoolgirl. I've just never seen it before because of that trick she has of hiding behind her hair. And she has skin like . . . like white violets in a cool shady secret place, velvety and untouched and just tinged with color.

White violets. He was a little surprised at the unexpected poetic image. But with those eyes and that skin it was perfect. White violets . . .

"You only want two things," she was saying, a bit defensively. "And I can't help you with either one of them."

"Really?" he said. "Two things? What two things?"

"To adopt Emily and Becky," she said. "And to buy back all the land that was part of the original Black Moon."

He drew Keno to a halt. Emmie and Becky were up ahead, romping their ponies back and forth in a field of bluebonnets. "Interestingly enough," he said, "you're right. It sounds as if you've been doing some research of your own."

"Yes," Laura said. "I have."

"Somehow I'm not surprised. What else have you found out?"

Laura took a deep breath. "You were born in Austin," she said. "You and Kit. You . . . you were ten minutes older than he was. In fact, you're the oldest of all your brothers and sisters."

The echo of his own voice, recounting his research that night on the deck in town, was unmistakable. "You make me sound positively ancient," he said.

"Not at all," Laura said. "You'll be thirty-six in a couple of months. The youngest is your brother Brian, who's twenty-two. There are ten of you. I'm sorry. Nine now, of course."

"You have been busy," he said dryly.

"You grew up on what was left of the Black Moon. It was started in 1868 by your great-great-grandfather, James Rafland. The legend is that on the night he first crossed Yegua Creek there was an eclipse of the moon, and that's where the name of the ranch came from."

"It's not a legend," Nick said. "It's true."

"I didn't say it wasn't," Laura said. "The Black Moon brand represents the eclipse. Two circles, dark and light. That's the symbol you have engraved on those cuff links you always wear."

Involuntarily he glanced down at his own wrists. Red cotton twill. Plain bone buttons. "Not always," he said.

She shrugged. "This is the first time I've seen you without them," she said. "After he settled in Texas, James Rafland married a Miss Harriet Nicholson. The Nicholsons were a prominent family in Lee County, and ever since then the first Rafland son's always been named Nicholson."

"I'm impressed," Nick said slowly. "You've found out things that—"

"I'm not finished yet," Laura said. "The Black Moon fell on hard times in the twenties and thirties. Your grandfather started selling off land to keep up his . . . rather sensational life-style. Your father did, too. By the time you and all your brothers and sisters were born, there wasn't much left but a few acres of scrubland. You didn't even have shoes except in the winter."

Nick looked at her thoughtfully. "Who on earth have you been talking to?" he said.

"I work for the newspaper, remember?" she said. "And I know the ladies in the Austin League. Your grandfather and your father were pretty colorful characters. So was your brother Kit. So's your mother. So's the rest of your family, for that matter."

"Colorful," Nick repeated. "Well, I suppose you could say that."

"And you," she said. "You, most of all."

He laughed. "How am I colorful?" he said. "I'm just an ordinary businessman."

"Oh, I think you're a little more than that," she said. "You're a working rancher and the guardian of two little girls and a hawk among the dovecotes of Austin's society hostesses and a spectacularly successful entrepreneur into the bargain."

"Me?" he murmured. "A hawk? Among the dovecotes? Obviously you're not very well acquainted with Austin's society hostesses."

Laura ignored him. "You and your Rafland Group," she went on, "are supposed to have an almost extrasensory knack for picking companies to invest in. It's a good thing, too, because according to the gossip you're obsessed with buying back all the land that was part of the original Black Moon. You have about half of it. What you want most of all is the old homestead itself, the section along Yegua Creek where James Rafland build his first house."

"The section," Nick said casually, "where we're standing right now."

She glanced at him sharply. "We're trespassing, then," she said. "Maybe we should go back."

He grinned at her. "How law-abiding you are," he said. "Relax, Miss Finesse. No one's going to shoot us on sight."

"And even if they try," she retorted, "you've come prepared to shoot back, haven't you? Varmints, indeed. I wouldn't think you'd want to teach the girls to disregard the law like this."

"The land's not fenced or posted," he said. "We're not doing any harm. In fact, we're going to have lunch up at the site of the old house. It's one of Emmie's and Becky's favorite places."

"Oh," Laura said. She didn't sound very happy about it.

Nick laughed. "It's all right," he said. "Really. The woman who owns the land knows perfectly well that we come here sometimes. Actually, I think she likes it when we do. She likes to taunt me with the fact that it's not mine."

"A woman owns it?" Laura said. "What woman?"

"I'm surprised you didn't find that out, too. In fact, I'm surprised that you didn't find out the... what was it? The titles of the books I borrowed from the library last week?"

She flushed again, and when she did he realized that he'd said it for just that reason: to see that faint white-violet color flood up under her skin once more. It looked so spontaneous. So fresh. It looked as if it would feel—

Then he remembered.

I really don't like it when you touch me. I really don't like it when anyone touches me.

What is the matter with me? he thought irritably. Whether it was fate or chance or just my own blind folly that afternoon at the Driskill, Laura Gardiner has been dropped into my lap like a gift from heaven. Emmie and Becky have adored her from the moment they saw her. And she's exactly what they need right now: a woman to care about them and show them new things, a woman with no other children to take her attention away from them.

So I suppose she is kind of a mother figure. Kind of a mom. But there's nothing make-believe about her. She's real. Genuine. I only wish she would...

What?

She's made it perfectly clear to me that she doesn't want to be touched. Why, then, do I keep thinking about touching her? Why do I keep thinking about wanting her, not only for Emmie and Becky, but for myself as well?

"I thought you should know what it felt like," she was saying. "Having someone pry into your life. And you should know by now that I'm not that easily distracted. Tell me about the woman who owns this land. The woman who likes to taunt you."

Nick took a deep breath. "Her name is Eleanor Kinnard," he said. "She's eighty if she's a day. She goaded her first husband into buying the land, back in the thirties. My grandfather needed the money, as usual, and Eleanor was out for revenge."

"Revenge? Why?"

"According to the old stories, she had a torrid fling with one of my...colorful great-uncles. It ended badly. She wanted to leave her husband but Jack Rafland wouldn't give up his carefree bachelor life and marry her. She never forgave him. She never forgave any of us."

"And she won't sell you the land because of that? That's not very fair."

"Fair," Nick said, "has nothing to do with it when you're trying to deal with Eleanor Kinnard. She's a fascinating old lady, Laura. The last of the Lee County belles. Capricious as hell and absolutely intent on getting her own way. I had a meeting with her about a month ago, and it didn't end on a very encouraging note."

"Why not?"

"Since she couldn't manipulate Uncle Jack into marriage," he said, "she's decided to start on me. I'm to go back and see her again when I've abandoned my wild bachelor ways and settled down."

She looked away. Her hair, caught in the clip, didn't fall forward across her cheek and hide her expression as it usually did. Her profile was thoughtful, even a little troubled. "Do you have wild ways?" she said.

"Why, Miss Finesse," he said. "I do believe you're shocked."

"No, I'm not."

"Yes, you are. And after all your research, you should know better. Oh, I suppose I might have had a wild way or two, once upon a time. But I learned—"

He stopped. Julie, he thought, all of a sudden, out of nowhere. My laughing accomplice in a thousand reckless devilments. Oh, yes, we had wild ways, Julie and I. Julie at five, Julie at twelve, Julie at sixteen. My friend, my confidante. My sweetheart. The beautiful fairy-tale princess I adored, when I was young. When she was young. When the whole world was young. God, I haven't let myself think about Julie for so long. Why here? Why now?

"I learned that wild ways wouldn't get me what I wanted," he said aloud. To his own surprise his voice sounded perfectly steady, even a little amused. "No, I don't have wild ways anymore. Eleanor just has a kind of undifferentiated grudge against Rafland men who refuse to get married. She'll open negotiations again, she says, when I can come back with a wife."

"That seems a bit drastic," Laura said.

"My sentiments exactly."

"So what are you going to do?"

"I don't know yet," he said lightly. "Maybe you and I could get married long enough for me to make an arrangement with her."

"Very funny," Laura said, after just an instant of hesitation. "And maybe Emily's Pegasus is going to sprout a pair of real wings and fly away home."

He laughed. "You cut me to the quick," he said. "I'll have you know that some of those society hostesses you were talking about consider me a nonpareil of eligibility."

"Marry one of them, then," Laura suggested unsympathetically. "Look. Emily and Becky have gone up over that rise."

"That's where the old house is," he said. "Well, since you don't seem to be interested in my impulsive but nonetheless heartfelt proposal, shall we go after them?"

She lifted her chin and smiled at him, the sudden lit-from-within smile he had seen so briefly in the Melrose Hall auditorium. "I'll race you," she said.

"Not fair," he said. "I have the baskets, and Keno—"

Whatever she did with her hands and her heels, it was too subtle for him to see. But Penny went from a standstill to an exuberant canter so quickly that he was left staring at nothing but Laura's slender back and the mare's rippling russet flag of a tail. Keno tossed his head and sidled, indignant at being left behind.

"Take it easy," Nick said, half to the big gelding, half to himself. "We'll never catch her now. But God, she is a beautiful creature, isn't she?"

And of course it was the borrowed chestnut mare he was talking about.

Wasn't it?

* * *

"Over there," Emily said, with as much gravity as a tour guide at the Smithsonian, "is the bunkhouse. It was far enough away from the main house that it didn't burn down in the fire. But it's pretty old, of course."

"I like it," Becky announced. "The cowboys slept there, and I'm going to be a cowboy when I grow up. If I ever run away from home I'm going to live in the bunkhouse. Just me and nobody else."

Laura put the last of the lunch dishes back in the basket. "That sounds kind of lonesome," she said. "Even for a cowboy. Nobody to talk to. Nobody to care about you, and nobody for you to care about. I don't think you'd like living all by yourself."

"Yes, I would," Becky said stubbornly.

"Nobody's going to run away from home," Nick said. He finished tightening Pegasus's girth and gave the white pony an affectionate slap on the rump. "Here, Laura, let me help you with those baskets. You sound as if you know what you're talking about. Living alone, I mean."

Laura handed him the panniers. "I'd never lived by myself until Aunt Grace died," she said. "She didn't believe in young ladies living alone, and of course after she had her stroke I had to be there. Now I'm all alone in the world for the first time in my life. It isn't that easy to . . . adjust, that's all."

He finished strapping the baskets behind Keno's saddle. "All of a sudden things are starting to make sense," he said thoughtfully. "Why you didn't just mail those papers back to me in the first place. Why you came out to the ranch that night. Why you came to the play, even when I asked you not to."

Laura walked over to where Penny was standing, long-legged and sleek and looking a little out of place in her English tack. "I thought you were glad I came," she said.

"I was," he said. "Once you got there. I just didn't understand why you were doing it. Come on, Emmie, sweetheart. Come on, Miss Lonesome Cowboy. Time to go."

From the homestead site on the rise they crossed the creek and rode northeast, through fields of new spring grass and a riot of wildflowers. At last they circled to the west and south and started back. The sun was beginning to sink and Laura could just see the line of brush that marked Yegua Creek when Emily screamed for the first time. In the huge flat openness it was a thin, almost unrecognizable sound.

Without stopping to think, Laura turned Penny toward the scream. The mare leaped forward. Nick already had Keno at a gallop, twenty yards in front of her. One of the picnic baskets broke free from the back of his saddle and spun crazily into the air.

Emily screamed again.

She was struggling with her white pony at the edge of a tangle of brush and an outcropping of weathered reddish gray rocks. Docile little Pegasus seemed to have gone mad, throwing his head up, crowhopping backward. In the grass at the pony's feet Laura caught a glimpse of something that looked like a fallen branch of a tree.

But there were no trees there. Only brush and rocks.

The branch moved, kinking sinuously through the grass.

Pegasus reared, striking out with his minute forefeet. Emily had lost her reins, her stirrups. She made a panicky little gasping sound and slipped helplessly out of the saddle.

Nick dragged Keno to a quivering standstill and swept the rifle out of the scabbard and dismounted, all in a single ruthlessly economical motion. Laura brought Penny to an abrupt halt behind him and held her motionless. She heard more hoofbeats coming up behind her: Becky.

"Don't move, Emmie," Nick said, in a calm conversational voice. "Just be still. Becky, stay back. Hold her, Laura."

Laura reached down for one of Snickers's reins. Emily had come to her knees in the grass. Her face was white but she was obviously too frightened to cry. She still had a mangled bunch of bluebonnets clutched in one hand.

"It's a snake, Uncle Nick," she said, in a tiny wavering voice. "A big one."

"I know, sweetheart," Nick said. "It's all right. Don't move."

He raised the rifle to his shoulder with an assurance so absolute that it looked almost nonchalant. The snake had gathered itself into a mottled spiral of dusty browns, its head raised, the insistent buzz of its rattles the only sound in the silence. Then the single shot exploded and the snake's coils whipped through the air and the buzzing stopped.

Snickers jumped backward so unexpectedly that the rein was torn from Laura's hand. Nick dropped the rifle and took one long step toward Emily and she threw herself into his arms with a hiccuping sob. Laura started to dismount. And then she realized that Snickers hadn't stopped, that his hoofbeats were drumming away too recklessly, too quickly.

She looked around, half in, half out of the saddle. The chocolate-colored pony was pounding headlong across the field toward the creek. Not for Becky, though, her sister's stricken panic. The tiny figure clung to the pony's back, and even at the distance Laura could see her dragging furiously at the reins.

Penny arched her neck and danced sideways. Laura pulled her around and regained her own balance in the saddle. She had a momentary blurred impression of Nick, down on one knee with Emily clinging blindly to his neck. Under his tan there was no color in his face at all, and with the bizarre clarity of crisis Laura read his thought, word for word: *I can never get back to Keno in time.*

"The creek," he said. "There's a bluff down there that drops off almost—"

Heels and hands and a shift of her weight, and Penny was off. Fat willful little Snickers, gorged with apples and cookies, was no match, of course, for Penthesilea, the legendary queen of the Amazons. But he had such a long lead. And every second took him closer to the line of brush that marked the creek.

I just have to turn them, Laura thought. That's all. I have to get to the creek first. You can do it, Penny. Oh, God, it's going to be close. It's going to be so close....

She flashed past the heaving, white-eyed pony. The bank of the creek was less than a hundred feet away. Too abrupt a turn, and Snickers would run right into them. Not enough of a turn and Penny, beautiful Penny, high-hearted Penny with her exquisitely vulnerable long legs, would go over the edge of the bluff herself.

A second left. Laura shifted her weight and shortened the right rein. Penny crashed through the brush and then, on the knife-edge of the bank, bent into the turn. The ground crumbled, fell away under her near hind hoof. Laura slackened the reins and threw her weight forward as if she were taking a six-bar fence and suddenly Penny was up and away and Snickers had turned, too, slowing, faltering, and they were paralleling the creek on blessedly solid ground.

"Becky!" Laura called. "Becky, can you pull him in now?"

"Miss...Finesse," Becky gasped. Her fists were knotted deep in the pony's mane. "I'll...try."

Snickers dropped back to an exhausted jolting trot. Laura reached down and seized one of his reins and dragged his head around, forcing him to a halt at last. Penny stopped, too, breathing hard, trembling with exertion and excitement.

"Becky," Laura said again. She slid out of the saddle and caught the little girl around the waist. Her own legs felt as if they were about to buckle under her. "Are you all right?"

"'Course...I am," Becky said stoutly. She managed a smile but her tiny knuckles were white. "It was just...a little gallop...that's all."

Laura bowed her head against Snickers's withers and started to laugh. It was the only way to keep from crying. Her knees shook, and even in the late-afternoon sunlight her hands felt icy. "A l-little gallop," she repeated. "Oh, Becky."

There were more horses behind her, a voice and a flurry of motion and an arm around her waist just in time to keep her from falling. "Hang on," said Nick's soft deep voice, close to her ear. "I've got you. Becky, are you all right?"

"Is Miss Finesse all right?" Becky countered. With the uncanny resilience of childhood she sounded bright and interested and already completely over her fright. "She looks like she's going to faint or something."

"I'm not going to faint," Laura said. "Let go of me."

"In a minute," Nick said. His body was warm and unshakable as a rock at her back. "Just relax. You do look a little unsteady."

"I'm all right," Laura said. "Let *go* of me. I want to check on Penny."

Nick leaned forward. She could feel his breath against her cheek. "You and Penny," he murmured. "Amazons, the both of you. Becky and Snickers could have taken a dangerous fall, you know."

He let her go. She took a step away from him but her legs still didn't feel normal. All of a sudden she was down on her knees in the grass, and the tears of shock and adrenaline-rush and overwhelming relief were escaping her control after all.

"Miss Finesse?" It was Becky. "Don't cry. I'm all right. Really."

"And Penny's all right, too." Emily, serious and practical, as usual. "Just a few scratches from the brush."

A small hand, patting her shoulder consolingly. Becky's voice again. "I know what. We'll get you some flowers, you and Penny both. That'll make you feel better. Come on, Emily."

Images, bright and a little distorted around the edges, disconnected. Emily, clutching a handful of bluebonnets, so dreadfully alone in the grass just inches from the snake's rearing head. Snickers, wild-eyed, out of control. The line of brush at the edge of the bank. Penny, falling. And Nick, lifting the rifle to his shoulder with such easy, deadly competence...

Laura covered her mouth with her hands, forcing back the beginning of hysteria. The world reeled. Eternity passed. Then Nick himself knelt down and put his arms around her.

"Hush," he whispered. He laid one hand softly in the curve at the back of her neck and pressed her face down against his shoulder. "Everything's all right. Thank God you were here."

"That s-snake," Laura said in a muffled voice. "You just shot that snake so *casually.* And Penny almost went over the edge. I felt it, Nick, I felt her start to fall."

"Hush," he said again. "It might have looked casual, but it wasn't. Not with Emmie just a few inches away. And Penny's all right. You held her. You turned her just in time."

He stroked her hair. His touch was gentle and impersonal, as if he were comforting a frightened child. And he felt big and reassuring and so wonderfully solid. Laura leaned against him and waited for her breathing to sort itself out, for her heartbeat to slow, for her arms and her legs to obey her own will again.

Under her cheek, the muscle and bone of his shoulder shifted. He laced his fingers together at the back of her head and tilted her face up to his. "Amazon," he said again.

They looked at each other. The warm coppery glint was showing in his eyes. Then he bent his head and kissed her very lightly.

She didn't move. She couldn't move.

When she didn't pull away, his touch changed. It stopped being impersonal. And yet it wasn't like the way Jeff had touched her at all. It wasn't rough or intimidating or insistent. It was slow. Speculative. It gave her an odd sense of incompleteness, of sheer physical expectancy. Against all her memories and all her convictions, despite the uneasiness that made her stomach tighten, Laura let her head drop back and closed her eyes. . . .

Something small and soft struck her between her shoulder blades. She jumped. Nick let her go and looked up, and at the same time there was a burst of gleeful little-girl laughter. Another missile bounced off her shoulder. Laura looked down. It was a spike of bluebonnets.

"We found *millions* of bluebonnets," Becky cried. "And dayflowers and wine-cups and morning glories. We made necklaces. See?"

She threw a garland over Laura's head. Emily came up and very carefully placed another garland around Nick's shoulders. The wine-cups and dayflowers and pale pink morning glories looked fragile and not quite real against his scarlet shirt, the breadth of his chest, his black hair and tanned skin. He laughed. Emily began tying one end of a long chain of flowers around his wrist.

"And some for Penny, too," Becky announced. She was tucking more flowers, pink and blue and golden, in the noseband of Penny's bridle. The mare stood quietly, her head lowered, her ears pricked, her eyes alive with interest and intelligence.

"Hold out your hand, Miss Gardiner," Emily said. "I want to put this around all of us."

Laura hesitated for just a moment, and then she held out her right hand. Emily twisted the flower garland around her wrist and tied it, and then began wrapping it around her own forearm. Nick laughed again.

"Now you're never going to get away from us," he said. "Are you feeling better?"

"Yes," Laura said. It was a little awkward to keep her hand from touching his, with only the length of three wine-cup stems between them. "I guess so. Nick. Listen. I was upset, that's all. I wasn't myself. I don't want you to think that I—"

"I know," he said. "It's all right. Never mind."

"Becky!" Emily said. "You, too. All of us."

Becky turned and her sister encircled her wrist with the last of the garland. Then Emily looked up. For once she was smiling, and her serious little face was glowing with triumph.

"There," she said. "Now we're all safe and together and happy."

Impulsively Laura reached out and put her arms around her. Nick moved with her, but not quite quickly enough. The flower stems between their wrists pulled apart.

"Miss Finesse!" Becky said accusingly. "You broke it."

Laura opened her arms farther and gathered up Becky as well. Both little girls' arms twined eagerly around her neck. Their hair felt like silk against her face, smelling of wildflowers and open air and no-tears shampoo. It was so good to hug them. For some reason she didn't quite understand she craved hugging, craved it fiercely, with every cell of her body.

"I'm sorry," she said. "I didn't mean to break your garland, Emily. I just wanted to hug you. Both of you. Oh, I just wanted to hug you more than I can ever say."

Chapter Four

"Laura Gardiner, please."

A confident, peremptory woman's voice. Laura cradled the telephone against her shoulder and kept on typing. Probably someone from the antique shop about Aunt Grace's bookcases and the chairs and the escritoire. It was about time they called.

"This is Laura Gardiner," she said.

"My name is Rafland," the woman said. "I believe you have been . . . seeing something of my son Nicholson."

Laura typed the rest of a word before she stopped. It actually took her a moment to connect Nick himself with the unabbreviated form of his name. "Well, yes," she said slowly. "I suppose I have. I hope there isn't anything—"

"No," the woman said. "There's nothing wrong. Nothing serious, anyway. Becky's had a small accident at school."

"A small accident?" Laura said sharply. "Where's Nick?"

"Nicholson is..." A peculiar little moment of hesitation. "He's in San Diego. Becky fell off the balance beam in her gymnastics class and sprained her wrist. We're here at Brackenridge in the emergency room, and she's got half a dozen doctors and nurses running around in circles. Screaming that she won't let them take an X ray unless you're here."

"Me?" Laura said blankly.

"You are Miss Finesse, I believe?" the woman said dryly. "The present Miss Finesse, I mean."

There was an echo of dislike, of old, old bitterness, in the way she said the name. But none of that mattered if Becky had been hurt. "I'm the only Miss Finesse at the moment," Laura said. "Tell Becky I'll be there in twenty minutes."

"Call me Nanfran," Nick's mother said. "My name is actually Nancy Frances, but as any fool can see I am neither a Nancy nor a Frances kind of a woman. And I can't stand being called 'Mrs. Rafland' in that excessively polite Miss Finesse voice of yours."

"How thoughtless of me," Laura murmured. "To inflict politeness on you when we don't even know each other."

Nanfran threw back her head and laughed. She was tall and angular, with a square strong-boned face and a mane of vigorous iron-gray hair brushed straight back and braided in a thick tail down her back. Her eyes were blue, but they had the same distinctive, faintly oblique setting that Nick's did.

"You've got gumption," she said. "And you certainly knew what to do to calm Becky down for that poor X ray technician. Nicholson told me about what happened last month at the Driskill, but I had no idea that you all had gotten so close."

"Nick and I," Laura said, "are not exactly close."

"No?" Nanfran leaned forward and looked at her curiously. All of a sudden her resemblance to Nick was more marked than ever. "How odd, then, that Becky was so anxious to have you here. That seems fairly close to me."

"I am close to the girls," Laura said. She had a momentary memory-flash of Nick kneeling in the grass by Yegua Creek, his eyes so dark, dark and warm, and his mouth... She suppressed the image abruptly and said, "Nick and I are just friends. Not even that, really. We have a kind of an arrangement."

"Ah," Nanfran said. Her blue eyes were uncomfortably direct. "An arrangement. I see. Well, Miss Laura Gardiner, you were willing to drop whatever it was you were doing and come straight over here when I called. So I'm going to do you a favor in return. I'm going to tell you the truth."

Laura frowned. "The truth about what?"

"The truth," Nanfran said, "about Nicholson."

"I already know—"

"No, you don't," Nanfran said. "Nicholson doesn't understand it himself, and now that Christopher's gone I think I'm the only person left who knows. The only person other than Julie."

"Julie?" Laura said uneasily. "A woman, and Nick? Oh, I don't think you should—"

"Nonsense," Nanfran interrupted again. "If you're going to be making... arrangements with Nicholson, young woman, you should know what you're getting into."

"It's not that kind of an arrangement," Laura said. "We just agreed that I would spend some time with the girls, that's all. I don't think he'd want you to tell me personal things about him."

"Nicholson is a romantic, you see," Nanfran went on, as if she hadn't even heard Laura's words. "Under that twentieth-century businessman's veneer of his, he's Don Quixote riding out alone to slay windmills."

"Windmills," Laura repeated thoughtfully. Unexpected as it was, it was a surprisingly apt allusion. "Yes. Or rattlesnakes."

Nanfran raised her eyebrows. "Becky told me about that," she said. "She also told me a hair-raising story about you almost going over the edge of a bluff when her pony ran away with her. I certainly hope Nicholson expressed a suitable gratitude."

The image again. Nick's eyes had been so dark, dark and warm, and the touch of his mouth so quick and so gentle but at the same time hinting at something that wasn't quick and gentle at all, something slow and languorous and shudderingly intense. Not gratitude. Oh, no, not gratitude...

All of a sudden Nanfran looked much too much like her son for comfort. Laura looked away. "He did," she said.

"Indeed," Nanfran said. There was a new note of interest in her voice. "How I wish I could have been there. The girls are part of it, you know. Nicholson's romantic code."

"Protecting them, you mean. Slaying any windmills that might threaten them."

"Figuratively speaking, of course," Nanfran said. "You should know what I'm talking about. He thought you were a windmill, that afternoon at the Driskill."

"Oh, yes," Laura said. "I know."

"His obsession with the ranch is another part of it. That was the only reason he started the Rafland Group, you know. The only reason he wanted to make money. To buy back his heritage. And she was part of it, too. Her name was Julie Harrow."

Laura said nothing. Don't tell me about her, she thought. She has nothing to do with me. Oh, please. Please. Don't tell me....

"Her name still is Julie Harrow, for that matter," Nanfran went on inexorably. "Julie Harrow McAllister, at least. She and Nicholson were what you might call childhood sweethearts. Both of them wild as the wind. But until they were twenty or so neither one of them so much as looked at anyone else."

Laura felt a small inexplicable pang of envy at the thought of Nick Rafland, twenty years old, wild as the wind, untouched and unscarred and passionately in love. She frowned. "What happened?" she said.

"The Harrows," Nanfran said, "were as poor as we were. Julie's mother was ailing all the time. She was a beautiful creature, I'll give her that. Julie, I mean. Hair as blond as a little girl's. Green eyes. It was no wonder George McAllister started taking an interest. And she couldn't ignore him."

"Why not?"

"Oil money," Nanfran said succinctly. "He may have been forty-something and he may not have been much to look at, but he was rich. Rich enough to send Mrs. Harrow up to the Mayo Clinic for the surgery she needed."

"But Nick—"

"Nicholson could buy and sell George McAllister ten times over," Nanfran said dispassionately. "Today. Fifteen years ago he didn't have a penny. And Julie was watching her mother die by inches. She and Nicholson agreed to break off their engagement. I think it almost killed her. I know it almost killed him."

Laura swallowed. "But still," she said. "It was all fifteen years ago. And Nick doesn't seem like a man who wouldn't be able to get over a girl he knew when he was twenty. No matter how much he may have... loved her."

"Oh, he got over her," Nanfran said. "Do you think he would allow himself to go on loving another man's wife? He even sees them occasionally. Social things. Charity things. Everyone's always very civilized. Very pleasant. And of course Nicholson has no objection to... feminine company of his own. But a romantic ideal of what it's like to be in love is a fragile thing. Once it's broken, it's broken. It can't ever be mended."

"Nanfran," Laura said desperately. "Why are you telling me this?"

"Mrs. Rafland?" An orderly was standing at the door of the waiting room. "We've finished with Becky. She's ready to go home."

Nanfran stood up. "Thank you," she said. Then she turned back to Laura. "I'm telling you this," she said, "because you came when Becky called for you. Because you could very well have saved her life the other day, out by the creek. So listen to me. No matter how much time he may spend with you, no matter how close you may be with the girls, no matter what kind of an... arrangement you may have, Nicholson will never fall in love with you. Never."

Laura came to her feet as well. "I don't want him to fall in love with me," she said.

"Good," Nanfran said coolly. "I just hope you're not going to change your mind about that."

The perfectly ordinary tan manila envelope was folded over and stuffed into the mailbox along with the telephone bill and a flyer from Wal-Mart. Laura frowned at it. From Southard and Sons, the antique dealers. What can they be sending me? she wondered. If they've finally sold Aunt Grace's furniture it wouldn't take an envelope this size to send me a note and tell me so.

The house certainly did look lighter and more welcoming without the looming dark mahogany bookcases and the four Duncan Phyfe side chairs and the escritoire. We should never have brought it all from Charleston, Laura thought, smiling to herself a little ruefully. We should have known we'd never have room for it. But Aunt Grace did love her furniture. And I am keeping the lamps and the dressing table, at least....

She tore the envelope open. There was a smaller brown envelope inside with strips of shiny old-fashioned cellophane tape crisscrossed at its corners. Paper-clipped to it there was a note on crisp white Southard and Sons stationery.

Dear Miss Gardiner:
We are pleased to inform you that we have found a buyer for your Queen Anne escritoire. In the course of displaying it to the customer, our representative discovered the enclosed envelope affixed to the underside of the writing surface. I hasten to assure you that we are simply forwarding the envelope to you without opening it or examining its contents in any way.

Yours very truly,
Jonathan Southard

With only the mildest of curiosity, Laura pulled the note free and opened the second envelope. The letters in it were yellowing around the edges. The name on the letterhead was vaguely familiar. Frederick Fournier, Esquire. An Edward Fournier had been the head of the old family law firm in Charleston that had handled Aunt Grace's affairs. Probably Frederick's son.

The first letter was dated September 24, 1963. It was addressed to Grace Gardiner in Charleston.

The year I was born, Laura thought. Do these old papers have something to do with me, with the adoption? If they do, why on earth would Aunt Grace hide them away as if they were a secret will or a murderer's confession in a mystery novel?

Still without any particular sense of foreboding she began to read the first letter.

My dear Grace:
I hope that you are feeling well and are not seriously endangering your health by returning to your employment so precipitously.

Laura Lavinia is safe and healthy at the Canfield-Gray Clinic in Sarasota. I assure you that the records of the birth have been permanently sealed, and even Dr. Gray himself is entirely unaware that you and the baby's mother are the same person. I am proceeding with the...

Laura stopped. She stared at the words.

You and the baby's mother are the same person...

The same person...

I must be reading it wrong, Laura thought blankly. It can't possibly say what it seems to say. It can't possibly say that Aunt Grace was...

...you and the baby's mother are the same person. I am proceeding with the "adoption," and I should be able to bring Laura Lavinia to Charleston within a few weeks. No one but you and I will ever have any reason to suspect that this has been anything other than a perfectly ordinary, straightforward legal transaction. However, if you will forgive the plain speaking of an old, old friend, I would like to implore you one last time to...

That Aunt Grace was...

Oh, my God. My *God.*

Aunt Grace was my mother. My real mother.

My real mother.

And she never told me. She *died* without telling me. All those years, all my life, through it all she was my real mother and she never *told* me, she never let me call her *Mother,* and she died, she died, she *died* without ever telling me the truth....

...implore you one last time to confide in Laura Lavinia's father and give him the opportunity to do what

I am still old-fashioned enough to consider to be the right thing. Under the circumstances I understand your reluctance, but it is hardly fair to the man or to your daughter for you to...

Laura flung the letters away from her as if they were suddenly alive or aflame or suffused with deadly poison. "No," she cried aloud. "*No.* It's not true. She wouldn't have. She loved me. She *loved* me. Oh, she wouldn't have *done* that to me."

In answer there was only silence. The letters drifted to the hardwood floor. *No one but you and I will ever have any reason to suspect that this has been anything other than a perfectly ordinary, straightforward legal transaction.*

It was true. It was true. It was all horribly true....

There was a knock on the door.

Laura came back to herself with a jolt.

She was lying on the love seat under the windows. Her head ached viciously and her throat was raw and her eyes felt hot and swollen. Go away, she thought wearily. Whoever you are, go away.

Again, the knock.

Had five minutes passed since she'd walked in the door and opened the envelope from Southard and Sons? Five hours? Or five years? Laura buried her face in one of the purple cotton cushions and willed herself back into oblivion.

Knocking, for the third time. It was sharper and more insistent. Something about the sound of it told her who it had to be. And he was probably going to stand out there and pound on the door all night. Laura stood up, took three furious steps across the living room, and threw open the door.

No surprise, considering the autocratic crispness of the knock. It was Nick Rafland.

"Go away," she said.

It was the first deliberate rudeness of her life. But she was not quite quick enough to commit a second and shut the door in his face. He put one hand on the doorframe and stepped into the room.

"God in heaven," he said. "Laura. What's the matter?"

"Nothing," she said. Her voice didn't sound like her own at all. "Go *away.*"

"Don't be ridiculous," he said. "Have you hurt yourself? Are you sick?"

Laura stared at him for a moment. He looked tense and tired, but there was genuine concern in his dark eyes and the curve of his mouth. At least someone was concerned for her. At least one other human being cared, even if it was a perfunctory caring that existed only because she was a useful mother figure, a make-believe mother to the two little girls he really loved. She gestured at the room and turned away.

"Oh, all right," she said. "Come in. No, I haven't hurt myself. And I'm not sick. What time is it?"

"Nine o'clock," he said. "I'm sorry to be so late. To come without calling first. But I just got back to town. My mother has the girls with her at the ranch and I wanted to thank you for what you did this afternoon before I went out there. I saw your lights and I didn't realize you'd be..." He hesitated.

"I wasn't asleep," Laura said. She sat down on the love seat again and picked up another one of the purple cushions. It couldn't hug her back, but at least it filled her arms. "You don't have to thank me. I did it for Becky. Sit down if you want to."

Apparently he didn't want to. He looked at the pieces of paper lying on the floor. Then he took the three steps across the room and crouched down in front of her. "Laura," he said gently. "What is it? You've been crying."

Laura clutched the cushion. "No, I haven't," she said.

He smiled very slightly. "Amazon," he said. "What is it, then, that you haven't been crying about?"

He's talking to me as if I were one of the girls, Laura thought. I should resent it. I should refuse to tell him anything. I am a grown woman, after all, not a child he can...

But even as she thought it she heard her own voice saying, with infuriating shakiness, "She was my m-mother."

He frowned. "Who was your mother?" he said.

"Aunt Grace."

"Of course she—" He stopped. "Do you mean that she was your real mother? Your birth mother? How do you know?"

"The letters," Laura said. "She had them hidden in her escritoire. The antique-shop people found them and sent them to me. Oh, *God.* I don't know why she even bothered to *keep* them if she never wanted to—"

"Shh," he said. "You can't be that sure about what she might have wanted to do with them someday. May I look at them?"

Laura pressed her face into the cushion and made a desolate shrugging gesture. There was silence for a moment, and then she heard the faint rustle of paper as he gathered up the letters. Then silence again. At last she lifted her head.

He had separated one letter from the rest and was looking at it thoughtfully. "Did you read all of these?" he said.

"No," Laura said. "Just the first one. After that..." She had to stop and swallow down the hot tightness that was rising again in her throat. "After that the rest didn't seem to matter."

He looked at her. There was something in his expression that she didn't understand at all. "You're not as alone as you think you are," he said. "Your father may very well still be alive, right there in Charleston."

"My *father?*"

One corner of his mouth twitched. "It does take two," he said.

"Thank you very much," Laura said bitterly, "for sharing that startling piece of insight." After the first rudeness, it seemed that subsequent ones were surprisingly easier.

"Aunt Grace never... In that first letter, the old lawyer begged her to... Nick, for God's sake. Does it... Does it say who he is?"

"No," he said. "But the lawyer knows. At least, he has some kind of a mysterious letter for you. Listen to this.

> Laura seems determined to marry the Calhoun boy in June, despite my objections. Naturally, if she marries she will want to have children of her own, and in that case I shall feel obligated to tell her about her father and the unfortunate weakness that runs in his family.
>
> You are aware, Edward, that I have had two small strokes in the past year. I would like to stress to you that if anything should happen to me, immediately upon her marriage Laura is to be given the sealed envelope I left with your father. It is not to be given to her under any other circumstances whatsoever, whether I am alive or dead. I still hope to persuade her—

"And she tried," Laura interrupted. "But of course in the end none of it mattered. I didn't marry him, did I?"

"No," Nick said gently. "You didn't. I wonder what she means by 'the unfortunate weakness' that supposedly ran in your father's family."

Laura hugged the cushion more closely. "Heaven only knows," she said. "Aunt Grace was a hundred years behind the times that way. She believed in what she called 'bad blood.' But I never married Jeff, and so I'll never know who my father was or whether his blood was good or bad. I'll never be anything else but absolutely alone in the world. I met that Edward Fournier person, you know, back in Charleston, after Aunt Grace died. He handled all the legal arrangements, everything to do with her estate. And he never said anything about an envelope. I'll never know."

"He hardly had to say anything," Nick said slowly, "if he'd been handling legal affairs of yours and your...aunt's, all along. You would have notified him if you'd gotten married."

"I'll never know," Laura repeated stubbornly. "It says right there. He was only supposed to give me the letter if something happened to Aunt Grace before I married Jeff. When Jeff was killed, she probably took the letter back."

"You were only eighteen. Would she have been so sure that you would never want to marry someone else someday?"

"I was the one who was sure," Laura said. "I didn't actually tell her what happened, but she must have—"

All of a sudden she stopped. I didn't tell Aunt Grace what happened that last night, she thought. But I was going to tell her. I would have told her, no matter how humiliating it would have been to me, no matter how devastating the scandal would have been when we called off the wedding. I would have told her, if the accident hadn't happened first. But with Jeff dead, so suddenly and shockingly, what had happened the night before hardly mattered anymore to anyone but me.

And none of this is any of Nick Rafland's affair, anyway.

"Aunt Grace must have known how I felt," she said. "That's all. She would have destroyed the letter."

"I wonder. There's only one way to find out for sure, you know. Call this Edward Fournier and ask him."

"Why would I want to do that? Even if he still has the letter, he isn't going to give it to me."

There was a pause. And then Nick said, "He would have to give it to you if you were married. Not just married to your Jeff. Married to anyone."

"But I'm not married," Laura said. "And I'm not going to be."

He looked at her for a moment. He looked at the letters again, one at a time. At last he dropped them on the table by the door as if they didn't matter anymore, walked across the room and sat down on the love seat beside her.

"Did Nanfran tell you where I was today?" he said.

Laura frowned. Whatever she had been expecting, it certainly wasn't a recap of the day's business activities. "She said you went to San Diego."

"Did she tell you why?"

"No. I just assumed that you were out there buying a company or something."

He smiled. "No," he said. "It wasn't a business trip. I went to San Diego to see Sharon Scott."

"Oh," Laura said, surprised. "You found her, then."

"I found her. For what good it did me. She refused to sign the papers."

"Nick. You can't mean that after all this time she wants Emily and Becky *back.*"

"I don't know what she wants," he said.

He added a soft savage epithet, a phrase that made Laura blink. "She did tell me," he went on after a moment, "that she didn't like the idea of her daughters being brought up by a man alone. That now that they were growing up they needed a woman in their lives. God, if I didn't know better I'd think my own sisters had been out there coaching her. Or someone. It sounded rehearsed. A perfect little speech."

"But who on earth would be coaching her? And why?"

"I don't know."

"If she's supposed to feel that way," Laura said, "why doesn't she just come back to Austin herself? Why doesn't she at least write or call?"

"I asked her the same thing. I think it scared her. Finally she said she'd been waiting for the right time. The right...circumstances. She said she'd be back in touch with me. And then she said someone was waiting for her and got up and walked out." His voice was so rigidly controlled that it was almost unrecognizable. "Short of violence, which I have to admit was an almost irresistible temptation, there wasn't a thing I could do."

Laura hugged the purple cushion hard against her heart. At least Aunt Grace didn't use me as a pawn in some cold-blooded game, she thought. She made a home for me. She brought me up. She did her best for me, I suppose, within the narrow bounds of what she thought was proper.

She just didn't love me.

If she had loved me, she wouldn't have left me without ever telling me the truth. If she had loved me, she would have told me who my father was, given me some vestige of a family, instead of leaving me with nothing in the world but a houseful of antique furniture and a tantalizingly untouchable sealed envelope.

A family, a family. Parents and brothers and sisters and children of my own like...

Emily, sweet Emily, so grave and shy and practical. Quicksilver imperious Becky, clinging to my hand this afternoon at the hospital. Their mother doesn't love them, either. But at least they had their father for a little while. And now they have Nick. Nick, who'll ride out and slay windmills to protect them.

"So what are you going to do?" she said aloud.

"I'm going to fight Sharon Scott through every court in the country if I have to," Nick said. His voice was his own again, deep and calm. "And I want you to help me."

"Me? How?"

"Laura," he said. "Listen. Are you all right? Can we talk about something serious?"

Laura took a deep breath. "Of course I'm all right," she said. "What?"

"This is going to sound a little strange at first, but hear me out. Do you see it? The connection between that letter your Aunt Grace left with her lawyer, and what Sharon Scott said to me out in San Diego?"

...immediately upon her marriage Laura is to be given the sealed letter I left with your father....

...She did tell me that she didn't like the idea of her daughters being brought up by a man alone....

"Yes," Laura said. All of a sudden her mind felt clear and sharp and as brittle as glass. "I see it. Of course I see it. It's being married. For both of us."

"Exactly," he said.

There was a moment of absolute silence. Neither one of them moved. At last Laura took a breath and said, "You seem to be suggesting that since we each have something to gain, and since neither one of us wants to get married to anyone else in any ordinary sense of the word, we should simply marry each other."

"There would be advantages for both of us," he said. His voice was still perfectly calm, as if he were discussing a merger between two of his handpicked business ventures. "You would have a stable, legitimate, ongoing connection with Emmie and Becky, which is something I think you want very much."

"Yes," Laura whispered. "I do."

"And you'd have the Thundering Herd as well."

"The what?"

He smiled. "The rest of my family," he said. "My mother. My brothers and sisters. You'd certainly never be able to say you were alone in the world again."

"The Thundering Herd," Laura repeated softly. "A family. And I'd be able to ask for the letter. I'd be able to find out who my real father was. Maybe even why Aunt Grace never… Maybe even more about Aunt Grace and why she did what she did."

"Maybe," Nick said.

"And you," Laura said. "You wouldn't be a man alone anymore. Sharon Scott wouldn't be able to use that against you."

"True."

"I really do love them, you know. Just for themselves. That's the most important thing."

"I know. And they love you. What Becky did this afternoon is all the proof I need of that."

"And of course," Laura went on thoughtfully, "there's always Eleanor Kinnard. Eleanor Kinnard and the Black Moon."

"Ah. You remembered."

"Mmm-hmm. Advantages, you said. For both of us."

"I'm trying to arrange another meeting with her next month. A wife would be—" He stopped. He seemed to be choosing his words very carefully. "A wife would be a desirable thing to have."

"Figuratively speaking," Laura murmured.

He looked at her steadily. He didn't move or make any attempt to touch her, but all of a sudden her skin contracted and roughened. "No," he said. "No, Laura. Not figuratively speaking."

She stared at him. A little at a time one coherent thought sorted itself out from all the rest.

He's not like Jeff at all.

Slender mercurial reckless Jeff, just my height. Jeff, with his blue eyes...blue-gray eyes...and fair hair...sun-streaked hair. Jeff, so studiedly chivalrous, so charming...so abruptly and frighteningly violent when he was thwarted.

Her hands started to shake, and she pressed them together in her lap. How hard it was to remember everything exactly. How far away Jeff seemed. But in any case, Nick Rafland, six foot four if he was an inch, with his black hair and his tanned skin and his faintly oblique dark eyes, was about as far from Jefferson Calhoun as a man could get.

"I...I didn't realize," she said, "that you were talking about...a real marriage. A *marriage* kind of a marriage."

"Emmie and Becky need stability," he said quietly. "And a lifetime is a long time. Yes, I'm talking about a marriage kind of a marriage. Is that so...unimaginable, between you and me?"

Maddening as it was, Laura could feel the blood hot in her cheeks. So he remembered that moment out by Yegua Creek as well. "I don't know," she said uncertainly. "That wasn't what I thought you meant. That makes it... different.''

He leaned back, almost as if he were deliberately giving her room to breathe, room to feel safe. The faintly speculative glimmer in his eyes might have been nothing more than a trick of the light. ''You don't have to decide just this minute, you know,'' he said. ''It's what, Tuesday? Let's have dinner this weekend and talk about it some more.''

''Nick, you don't understand. I don't know if I can—''

''Shh,'' he said. ''Don't say no yet. Think about it.''

''You've already made up your mind, haven't you?''

''Why do you say that?''

''There's one more advantage on your side of all this. An important one. One that you didn't mention before.''

He frowned a little. ''What?'' he said.

A romantic ideal of what it's like to be in love is a fragile thing, Nanfran had said. *No matter what kind of an arrangement you may think you have with him, Nicholson will never, never fall in love with you. Never.*

''You can sit there and ask me to marry you, cool as you please,'' Laura said. ''And you don't even have to pretend that you're in love with me.''

Chapter Five

"I've been thinking about it," Laura said. "Ever since Tuesday night. And it's a preposterous idea. A marriage of convenience, for heaven's sake. People just don't do things like that in the twentieth century."

Nick scooped up a teaspoonful of Chuy's homemade red salsa on one point of a tortilla chip. "People do all kinds of preposterous things in the twentieth century," he said mildly. "They even hang hubcaps from the ceilings of Mexican restaurants."

"I like Chuy's," Laura said. "It's fun. And the food is wonderful."

He ate the chip with the salsa. It didn't drip, not one tiny bit. Typical Nick. "I like it, too," he said. "Hubcaps and all. It's just not what I was expecting when I asked . . . Miss Finesse to choose a restaurant for dinner on Saturday night."

"And what were you expecting?"

"White damask tablecloths," he said. "Fresh flowers. Three or four forks."

"If that's the only thing you want in a wife," Laura said, "this whole thing is an even bigger mistake than I thought it was."

He smiled. "Somehow I can't quite picture Emmie and Becky coping with four forks," he said. "Of course that's not the only thing I want in a wife."

Laura toyed with a chip. "This feels strange," she said. "We don't even *know* each other, not really. And you're talking about what you want and don't want in a wife."

"What I want," he said, "is you."

The chip snapped in two. Laura bent her head, just enough to allow her hair to fall forward across her cheek.

"Don't blush," Nick said calmly. "I didn't mean that in any...ungentlemanlike personal sense." There was the very faintest tinge of self-mockery in his soft deep voice. "At least, not just at the moment, right here in a front booth at Chuy's. Let me rephrase it. In fact, let me amend it a bit. What I want in a wife, bigamous as it may sound, is both of you."

"Both of me?" Laura shook back her hair and looked up. "What on earth do you mean by that?"

"Miss Finesse," he said, "with her ice-cream-cone etiquette and her four-fork place settings, does have a certain civilized charm. A certain . . . formality. I can think of moments when I would be absolutely delighted to be married to Miss Finesse."

"Your meeting with Eleanor Kinnard, I suppose," Laura said tartly. It was perfectly true, of course, and that was just what made it so intensely annoying. "I'm not that formal."

"Not always," he said. "Every so often I get the impression that there's someone else hiding inside that cool proper Southern lady. A woman who laughs as if she has a light shining through her. A woman who has a positively voluptuous collection of purple cushions on her love seat and a sock under her dining room table. A woman who likes Chuy's on a Saturday—"

"A *sock?*"

"It's amazing what one notices when one is down on one's knees gathering up old letters from the floor."

"For heaven's sake, Nick, you make it sound as if I never cleaned house at all."

Aunt Grace's voice, chiding, out of the past: *You were born with a hedonistic and disorderly nature, my dear, and you must always struggle against it. Never forget that you are a lady....*

Born with it, Laura thought, with a flash of new awareness. I must have heard her say that a thousand times, and I never realized... She always said I was *born* with it. Was that what my father was like? Hedonistic and disorderly?

Why did she love him, then?

"Laura?"

She blinked. Across the table, Nick Rafland was looking at her with a faintly questioning smile. "One stray sock," he said mildly, "is hardly squalor. Actually, I thought it was...rather endearing. I'm sorry I sounded as if I were criticizing."

"No," she said. "That's not what I was thinking. I was thinking about...about love."

He leaned back in the booth, and his smile faded. "Love again," he said. "Laura, I—"

"No," she said, cutting him off. "Not you. It's all right. I don't expect you to love me. I don't want you to love me."

"But I will care for you," he said quietly. "In my own way. I suspect that my mother whiled away the time at the hospital on Tuesday entertaining you with her story of me as Sir Lancelot."

"Actually, it was Don Quixote."

"Close enough. It's not really true, you know."

Nicholson doesn't understand it himself, Nanfran had said. *Now that Christopher's gone I think I'm the only person left who knows. The only person other than Julie...*

"Not true?"

"Oh, the details are true enough. Yes, I was going to marry Julie Harrow. Yes, she married George McAllister instead. And yes, I suppose it more or less made it impossible for me to...fall in love again, in the adolescent romantic sense. But I'm certainly not the storybook heartbroken cavalier she makes me out to be. I don't think anyone ever falls in love like that, more than once."

The detachment in his voice was so perfect that it couldn't possibly be real. Nanfran had been right, then. *Nicholson doesn't understand it himself....*

"I don't know," Laura said. "I've never been in love like that at all."

"No?" he said. "I would have thought that you and your fiancé—"

"No," she said. "I wasn't in love with Jeff. I thought I was, at first. But I wasn't. I found out that I wasn't."

He frowned. She could almost see him sorting back through the things she'd said to him, the things she'd done, rearranging them, searching for a new pattern. "Did you find out," he said slowly, "that you didn't want him to touch you, either?"

Jeff's hands hard on her arms, his fingers digging into her flesh. His mouth, rough, unthinking, voracious. A black flash as she fell, and then what seemed like endless sick frantic helplessness ... Afterward, his voice, the voice of a stranger: *You're not normal, Laura, do you know that? You're not even human. No flesh-and-blood woman could ever be as cold as you've been with me, from the very beginning....*

Laura closed her eyes and swallowed back scalding bitterness. "It doesn't matter," she said. "It was all so long ago."

"I think it does matter."

She opened her eyes and looked at him. "Oh, I suppose it does," she said. "I suppose it matters to you if you still want to go through with this marriage thing."

"I want to go through with it."

"Right away?"

"I don't know what Sharon Scott is going to do or when she's going to do it. Yes, I want to get married right away."

"What will you tell the girls?"

He smiled. "In case you haven't noticed," he said, "the girls have been matchmaking their little fingers right down to the bone from the very beginning. They'll be delighted. Anyway, at their age they expect grown-ups to do strange things."

"I just signed a new lease on the house. My house."

"You could sublease it."

"I won't give up my job."

"I haven't asked you to."

"The girls are in school during the year, anyway," Laura said, half to herself. "And I could work at home sometimes, if I wanted to. A lot of the columnists do that."

"So do I. We could work it all out together."

"And so it just keeps coming back to... to the fact that I don't want... that I don't like it when you touch me."

"I think," Nick said gently, "that we could work that out together, too."

Laura picked up a tortilla chip and began to break it into pieces. All right, she thought. Calm down. Think this through.

He's intelligent. A piece for intelligence. A piece for honesty, and one for calm steadiness and one for sensitivity. Almost too much sensitivity, sometimes.

A piece for...well, for being tall, dark-haired, dark-eyed, so different from Jeff. A piece for being willing to ride out and slay windmills, however much he might deny it. A tiny, tiny piece just for having such an appealing smile.

And then, of course, there are the girls. That's the biggest piece. Sometimes when I close my eyes I can still see the three of them, standing on the veranda out at the Black Moon, Nick with Emily and Becky on either side of him, the caring and the kinship like a circle of light around them.

I can go into that circle after all. He's inviting me inside.

And there's Aunt Grace's letter, too, lying all these years in some dusty file in Edward Fournier's office. The last piece of the chip, an odd-shaped, sharp-edged piece but a piece just the same, for a chance to read the letter.

"Can we wait a little while?" she said slowly, without looking up.

Intelligence, honesty, sensitivity. He knew what she meant, of course. "We can wait," he said. "If that's what you want. Although I do wonder..."

He hesitated for so long that she had to look up. In the deepest depths of his eyes she could see a tiny spark of copper. "What?" she said.

"I do wonder what might have happened," he said very softly, "if you and I had been alone that afternoon out by Yegua Creek."

Laura looked at herself in the mirror. Then she turned around and looked at herself again, over her shoulder. They're all expecting Miss Finesse, she thought, Nanfran and Nick's brothers and sisters. The Thundering Herd. Should I be wearing a skirt instead of jeans? That linen jacket instead of just my white shirt and my lucky purple suede vest? Oh, God, purple again. I didn't realize that I had so much purple everywhere.

What am I going to say to them? What are they going to think?

I haven't even seen Nick himself for a whole week, since we had dinner at Chuy's last Saturday night. Everything's been arranged by phone, so sensibly, so impersonally. *A barbecue on Saturday at my mother's house.... I want you to meet them. Yes, I've told them... We'll be married at the ranch on the twentieth. Judge Martin Nicholson, who's a cousin of mine...*

The doorbell rang. Laura's stomach lurched faintly. But the cottage was so tiny that a dozen steps would take her from the bedroom to the front door, and there was really no excuse for lingering. She looked around. Everything looked just the same as it always did. Warm. Colorful. Neat. Well, fairly neat. No socks on the floor, at least.

It's amazing what one notices when one is down on one's knees gathering up old letters from the floor....

All of a sudden she stared at her own comfortable haphazard living room as if she had never seen it before. It was clean enough, but it wasn't really neat at all. It certainly didn't look like white damask tablecloths, fresh flowers, and three or four forks. It didn't have a certain civilized charm. Now that Aunt Grace's furniture was gone it didn't look like Miss Finesse at all. It looked like the real Laura, like Laura-on-the-inside. It looked like...almost like a *mom,* for heaven's sake. Had it always been there, the warmth, the color, the casualness? Did I just never see it, Laura thought, all through the years, because Aunt Grace's furniture was so formal and there was so much of it and she always wanted it just so?

Hedonistic and disorderly...

Laura took a deep breath. She picked up her purse. Then she opened the door, stepped outside and closed the door firmly behind her.

Nick Rafland took a single quizzical step backward. The week hadn't changed him. He was as tall as ever. His skin was still neatly tailored over the sharp, distinguished bones of his face, and his smile was still quick and white and tinged with a hint of secret self-mocking amusement at his own shortcomings. Whatever they might be. Because Nick Rafland, casual and immaculate in faded jeans and a crisply pressed cotton shirt, appeared to have no shortcomings at all.

The shirt was pink.

More than pink. It was an extravagant rosy golden color, about the shade you'd get if you rubbed a flamingo with apricots. Assuming, of course, that you could get the flamingo to stand still long enough. It was startlingly effective with his tanned skin and black hair and oblique dark eyes.

Laura blinked at him. "Pink?" she said.

The moment the word was out of her mouth she thought, Pink? *Pink?* Is that the best you can do? You haven't seen him for a week and you're going to marry him in another two weeks and the best thing you can think of to say to him is *Pink?*

He grinned at her. "I like to think of it as terra-cotta," he said. "It's one of my secret vanities. Good morning."

She felt herself flush. First I don't invite him in, she thought, and then I blurt out *Pink?* as if I think he's wearing a ballet tutu or something. Aunt Grace would swoon on the spot. "Good morning," she said politely.

"Do you have a hidden body in there?" he asked mildly. "Or a clandestine gambling casino?"

"Of course not."

"A renegade band of marauding socks?"

"Don't be ridiculous," she said. "Where are the children?"

"I took them out to Nanfran's last night," he said. "I wanted to have a few private minutes with you this morning."

"Nanfran?" Laura said. "You call her that, too?"

"She's liable to take a horsewhip to anyone who tries to call her something she considers mawkishly sentimental. Like 'Mother' or 'Grandmother.' Or even 'Mom.'"

"She's a little... daunting, isn't she?"

"That's the whole point," Nick said. "Nanfran adores daunting people. She's looking forward to seeing you again, though. I think she's expecting you to correct everyone's table manners at lunch. If you're ready, we should probably go."

"What did you want to have a few private minutes with me about?"

"It's in the car," he said.

They walked down the sidewalk. The car was a black sedan, something Laura didn't recognize, its unobtrusively elegant shape tapering gracefully front and back, its deep gleaming finish almost liquid in the glare of the sun. He opened the door and she got in. The car was pale gray on the inside, and it smelled faintly of leather and newness.

"What?" she said again, when he got in on the other side.

He opened the console between the seats and took out a small square box covered with faded violet moiré silk. "This," he said.

Laura hesitated for a moment, and then she took it from him. It was quite obviously a jeweler's box, and from its size it probably contained a ring. "You didn't have to do this," she said slowly. "After all, we're not really...not really..." Not really what? she thought. Her voice trailed off uncertainly.

"We are getting married," he said softly. "Really. Whatever our...reasons or our private arrangements may be, you are going to be my wife. There's a ring in that box that means a great deal to me, and I'd like you to wear it."

She forced her hands to steadiness and opened the box. It wasn't a diamond. It wasn't new or expensive or showy at all. It was an oval moonstone set plainly in thin old platinum, surrounded by small polished cabochon amethysts.

"A moonstone," she said. "An old one. Oh, Nick, it's lovely."

"Moons," Nick said, "of various sizes and shapes and colors, seem to run in the Rafland family. My great-great-grandfather had that ring made for Harriet Nicholson back in 1870."

She waited, but he made no move to take the ring and put it on her finger. After a moment Laura picked up the ring herself and slipped it on. The fit was improbably perfect.

"There's a wedding ring that goes with it," Nick said. "Just a plain band. And there's...well, there's something else that I'll show you some day, too. Do you like it?"

"Yes," Laura said. Her throat was tight, and she wasn't quite sure why. The moonstone glimmered on her finger, clear as a drop of water and at the same time alive with translucent pearly blues and violets. "Thank you," she ıdded, in a small cool formal voice. "It's beautiful, Nick, ınd I like it very much indeed."

"The rest of you may be excused now," Nanfran said, with an imperious wave of her hand. "I want to have a little visit with Miss Gardiner here."

Peremptory as it was, no one argued. Of course, Laura hought uneasily, from what Nick says no one ever argues with Nanfran. The members of the Thundering Herd all stood up immediately, murmured a few pleasantries and drifted away. Nick himself, lounging casually on Laura's ight, was the only one who didn't move.

"You, too, Nicholson," Nanfran said. "I certainly don't want you hanging on our every word while Miss Gardiner and I get to the bottom of this whole peculiar business. Go away."

Nick didn't get up. "Miss Gardiner?" he said. "Are you n the mood to be gotten to the bottom of?"

"I think I can probably manage," Laura said. "Mr. Rafland."

"See?" Nanfran said tartly. "She doesn't need you to ake up for her. Now scoot."

The mental picture of Nick Rafland's six-foot-four-inch rame scooting anywhere under any circumstances at all was so ludicrous that Laura had to force down a nervous giggle. Nick did laugh, and then after a moment he stood up.

"All right," he said. "I'm going. I think it's about time I checked on Emmie and Becky, anyway."

"Well, Laura," Nanfran said, when he had gone. "So you're going to be part of the family now. A new... arrangement. Have you been enjoying yourself today?"

"Yes, I have," Laura said politely. "Very much, thank you. You were doing it just to annoy him, weren't you? Calling me 'Miss Gardiner' like that."

Nanfran grinned. "There aren't many people who're willing to stand up and annoy Nicholson these days," she said. "It's good for him. So what is it? Are you pregnant?"

For a moment Laura looked at her silently. It's at times like this, she thought, that I really appreciate all of Aunt Grace's day-in-and-day-out discipline. How else would I know the exact degree of cool disdain a lady uses to answer a question like that?

"No," she said. Coolly. Disdainfully.

"Is it the money?"

That was a little more unexpected. "The money?" Laura said. "What money?"

"Don't be naive," Nanfran said sharply. "The Rafland Group and the Black Moon represent a great deal of money."

"I've supported myself all my life," Laura retorted. "And taken care of my...of my Aunt Grace as well. I never even thought about the money and I don't care whether you believe it or not."

Nanfran laughed. "I like you, Laura Gardiner," she said. "All right. You're not pregnant and you don't care about the money. So let's stop playing games with each other. I know why Nicholson's doing this, of course. He told me about his little confrontation with Sharon Scott in San Diego. And I've always known about Eleanor Kinnard and her idiotic grudge against Rafland men who won't get married. Oh, yes, from Nicholson's point of view it makes perfect sense. What doesn't make sense to me is why you're willing to... accommodate him."

She waited expectantly. Laura said nothing.

"Part of it, I suppose, is the children," Nanfran continued thoughtfully. "Emily and Becky adore you, and you quite obviously feel the same way about them. But you're a young woman. A very attractive young woman. You could certainly find a husband in a... more traditional way, and have children of your own."

"I don't want to find a husband in the traditional way. When I met Nick I wasn't looking for a husband at all."

"What were you looking for, then?"

Laura turned away and looked across the lawn. Emily and Becky were down by the creek, playing with a swarm of cousins. Nick was leaning against a tree, watching. One of his brothers and two of his sisters were standing with him, talking, laughing. All around them there was the casual ease of shared blood, shared memories.

The circle again. The circle of light. Family. Belonging. Acceptance...

"You haven't answered my question, young woman."

"I was all alone," Laura said. The children were playing statues. A boy was swinging Emily around, and she was shrieking with uncharacteristic laughter. "I was looking for you."

"For me?"

"For you, plural. For the girls, of course. But for all the rest of you, too."

"The family?" Nanfran said. "Well, that at least makes some sense, I suppose. Don't you have anyone of your own?"

Naturally, if she marries she will want to have children of her own, and in that case I shall be obligated to tell her about her father....

"No," Laura said. "Not now. Not yet."

"Laura. Look at me."

Laura turned her head. Nanfran had that intent curious expression on her face again, the expression that made her look so much like Nick despite her blue eyes and gray hair. "Do you remember what I told you?" she said. "He's not going to fall in love with you."

"I remember," Laura said.

"But once you're his wife, you're going to be important to him. Don Quixote, remember? The knight and his lady."

"I know. I won't disappoint him."

"Humph," Nanfran said. Her voice sounded just a little husky. "See that you don't."

"See that she doesn't what?" Nick's soft deep voice said from behind them. Laura jumped, and he put one hand lightly on her shoulder. "You seem to be holding your own," he said.

Laura sat perfectly still under his touch. After a moment he took his hand away. "We've been talking about you," she said.

He laughed. "I can imagine," he said. "Do you think you can tear yourself away from that fascinating subject? Becky says her wrist is starting to ache, and I'd like to take them home."

"Of course," Laura said. She stood up.

"Wait a minute," Nanfran said. "When are you planning to have this wedding of yours, Nicholson?"

"Two weeks from today," Nick said.

"Here, I presume."

"Or over at my house. I've asked Martin Nicholson to come out and marry us."

"Here," Nanfran said emphatically. "And all the family, of course. What about you, Laura? You'll want to invite your... well, your friends, at least."

"I'd rather have everything very quiet."

"How proper of you. And how exceedingly dull." All at once there was a spark of mischief in Nanfran's blue eyes. "I think I'll just make one or two little arrangements of my own, then. This is an occasion, after all. Nicholson, of all people, getting married at last. I want you two to have a wedding that no one in Texas will ever forget."

"What do you think she meant by that?" Laura asked, as they walked out to the car. Emily and Becky were skipping in front of them, laughing. "A wedding that no one in Texas will ever forget?"

"I have my suspicions," Nick said. "And it's not something I'm looking forward to. Some of the Black Moon wedding traditions go back a century or so."

"What do you—?" Laura began.

"We're going to be in the wedding," Becky warbled, dropping back beside them. The bandage on her wrist looked grubby after all the food and the games. "Emily and me. Aren't we?"

"Yes, my sweetheart, you are," Nick said. "Both of you. And you're going to have beautiful new dresses. Maybe Miss Laura will take you shopping sometime during the week."

"Yes!" Becky crowed. "Yes, yes. Please, Miss Finesse?"

"Please?" Emily added shyly.

"Of course," Laura said. "Whenever you want to."

Nick opened the back door of the car. "In you go," he said. "We'll be on our way in a minute. No, Laura, wait."

Laura paused, her hand on the gleaming chrome handle of the car's front door. "Hmm?" she said.

"Everyone's watching us," he said. "This has been more or less an engagement party, you know. And all day I think they've been waiting for some token show of affection."

Suddenly the handle felt cold under her fingers. No, it felt hot. Laura took her hand away. "A what?" she said.

"You heard me."

"Nick. Stop it. We agreed that we would—"

"Laura," he said. "We're standing in the driveway at my mother's house with Emmie and Becky in the car and about twenty people hanging on our every move. Turn around."

She turned. He smiled at her. Then he bent his head and kissed one corner of her mouth very gently.

She didn't move. She felt nothing at all, no tremor, no softness, no response.

"You have to do your part, too," he said softly. He kissed the other corner of her mouth. "I think you should put your arms around me."

Since she wasn't feeling anything, it didn't matter. Laura lifted her hands. The sleeves of the apricot-flamingo shirt were crisp and smooth under her fingers. She could feel the heavy muscles of his arms and shoulders under the cloth. They tensed and shifted. He brought his own hands up and put them on either side of her face and kissed her full on the lips.

A rush of sensation cascaded down through her body, flickered like lightning into her legs, flooded up into her throat. Her lips parted, shocked, gasping, and for just a moment his breath filled her mouth, clean and hot.

She made an incoherent sound and jerked away. He didn't try to hold her. They looked at each other.

"Don't do that again," she said. "Don't *ever* do that again."

"How emphatic you are," he said softly.

"We agreed. We *agreed* we were going to wait."

"I know," he said. He closed his eyes briefly and took a deep breath. "I know. I'm sorry. But it was only a kiss, my Amazon."

Silence. Laura looked down. Her hair fell forward and veiled her face, and it gave her some small vestige of privacy. She could feel the weight of the moonstone on her finger. "I know," she said at last. "I'm sorry I snapped at you. It was my fault, too."

"Do you want to change your mind?" he said. "About the marriage, I mean."

Emily and Becky, skipping and laughing. *We're going to be in the wedding....* Sharon Scott's mysterious threats. Eleanor Kinnard and the Black Moon. Aunt Grace's letter. "No," she said. "Of course not. Do you?"

He hesitated. And then he said, "No."

She waited for a moment or two more until she was sure she could face him. At last she shook back her hair and looked up.

"Then you'd better kiss me again," she said steadily. "So all the people who're watching us don't think we're having a fight."

"You're not serious."

"Of course I'm serious. Kiss me again."

He leaned forward and kissed her cheek. His lips were cool and somber. The lightning feeling flickered very faintly, far away, a remnant of a storm that had passed over and gone.

Gone...

"There," Nick said. His voice was cool and somber, too. "That should satisfy everyone that we're not having a fight."

"I certainly hope so," Laura said briskly. "Now. Let's take the girls home and see if we can't figure out a way to defend ourselves from this wedding that Nanfran says no one in Texas is ever going to forget."

Chapter Six

"You aren't dressed right," Becky said critically.

"You should be wearing a white dress," Emily said.

"A lo-o-ong white dress." Becky swept her arm out behind her. She had a fresh new bandage on her wrist, a smaller one, pristinely white itself. "Silk and satin and lace and stuff. And one of those puffy things on your head."

"A veil," Emily said. "And flowers to carry. A big, big bouquet of white flowers."

Laura smoothed her skirt a little self-consciously. It was plain tailored silk faille with a decorously cut jacket to match, all in an unassuming pale heliotrope color. Perfect for a quiet wedding at home. Ladylike. Conventional.

I hate it, Laura thought. It looks like something Aunt Grace would have worn. After today, I'm going to put it away in the very back of my closet and never wear it again.

"Not all weddings are like that," she said. "It wouldn't be appropriate for me to dress up so much, to wear a long white dress and a veil when—"

When there've been deaths in the family so recently, she thought. It's been less than four months since Kit was killed. Since Aunt Grace died. But the girls are so happy today. I can't say that to them. And I can't very well tell them that this isn't a long-white-dress kind of a wedding. That I'm only marrying Nick because we both have something to gain from it. That we don't really love each other at all . . .

"—when we're getting married so quietly," she said. "Here at home, with just the family, and no fuss."

"It's not too much fuss for you to walk on our rose petals, is it?" Emily asked anxiously, clutching her white straw basket with both hands. "Nanfran said it was good luck if you do. I want you to step on every single one."

Laura knelt down and hugged them, one with each arm. "No, honey, it's not too much fuss for me to walk on your rose petals," she said. "Yours, and Becky's, too. And I will step on every single one of them, even if it takes me all afternoon. I promise. Now, you'd better run on downstairs. It's time."

When they were gone, she stood up slowly. Again she smoothed her skirt, and the milky-clear glimmer of the moonstone caught her eye. She looked at it for a moment. Then she took it off and slipped it on the third finger of her right hand. It felt strange. And her left hand felt oddly light and bare and incomplete.

There's a wedding ring that goes with it. Just a plain band . . .

Laura took a deep breath and walked out of the room.

"Am I really all that terrifying?" Nick murmured, under the noise of the party.

It was over. The plain band was on Laura's finger, and the moonstone was with it, back where it so surprisingly seemed to belong. Nick's hands had been cool and matter-of-fact. That was all she really remembered, Nick's hands and the unexpected steady clarity of her own voice and the all-too-sudden moment when it was done and Nick had bent his head and kissed her very lightly, almost but not quite on the lips.

"Of course you're not terrifying," Laura said. "What on earth are you talking about?"

"You didn't seem quite able to walk a straight line when you came across the living room," he said. "What were you doing upstairs, fortifying yourself for your ordeal with Nanfran's bottle of medicinal brandy?"

"Don't be ridiculous." She shook her hair back and looked up at him. "You did kiss me, for heaven's sake. Did I taste as if I'd been fortifying myself?"

He smiled. "It was hardly that kind of a kiss," he said.

"It would hardly have to be that kind of a kiss," she said severely, "for you to tell if I'd been nipping into the brandy. For your information I wasn't trying to walk a straight line. I was trying to step on all the rose petals."

"You were what?"

"Your mother told the girls it was good luck for me to step on all the rose petals. And Becky was so excited that she was throwing them everywhere. I thought I'd never get all of them."

He started to laugh. "And I thought I might have to stop the wedding and call for black coffee," he said, "when I saw you in that very sedate and ladylike little suit, weaving all over the room and watching every step you took so carefully."

"I wasn't *weaving,*" Laura protested. And then all of a sudden she laughed, too. "Oh, all right, I suppose I was. But Emily in particular was so anxious about me stepping on all the petals. I wasn't thinking about what it looked like to everyone else."

"You are a walking talking mass of contradictions, Mrs. Rafland."

Laura frowned a little. *Mrs. Rafland.* It was true, of course, but it sounded so strange and so irrevocable, as if she weren't even herself anymore. "Why do you say that?" she demanded.

"Don't glower at me," Nick said. "This is our wedding ay, you know, and we're supposed to be deliriously happy. isten. I have a suggestion."

"I'm afraid to ask," Laura said.

He grinned at her. "So you do think I'm terrifying, after ll," he said. "Well, in this case you may have a point. Have ou ever heard of something called a shivaree?"

"Ye-es," Laura said tentatively. "It was a kind of a celbration they had at weddings in the Old West, wasn't it? verybody standing around outside the poor newlywed ouple's bedroom window and banging on pots and pans nd ringing cowbells and things like that."

"I should have known," he said, "that Miss Finesse vould be an expert on wedding customs, past, present and uture. But you're mistaken about one thing."

"What?"

"On the Black Moon," he said, "the shivaree is not necssarily a quaint historical curiosity."

"Nick!" she said. "Is *that* what Nanfran meant?"

"It would surprise me if it weren't," he said. "You should ave seen the melee when Brian got married last year. And ight now everybody has that same look, as if they know omething we don't. I think you and I should slip away beore we find ourselves in the middle of something a lot more ambunctious than a few stray rose petals."

Laura put her champagne glass on the table. "I'll go get mily and Becky," she said.

He laid one hand on her arm. His touch was very light nd casual, but at the same time there was something new n it, the faintest flavor of privilege, of possessiveness. Laura urned and looked at him and all of a sudden it struck her vith a physical force that went beyond all the marriage cermonies and all the plain platinum bands in the world: *I am his man's wife.*

A frightening uneasiness stirred in her throat, her stomch.

"Are you all right?" Nick said. He had not taken his hand away. Laura could feel each of his fingers separately and distinctly through the silk faille of her sleeve.

"Yes," she said automatically.

"It's just that Emmie and Becky are staying here," he said. "Along with half a dozen assorted cousins. Another one of Nanfran's contributions to our first night of... wedded bliss. I couldn't very well tell her that we didn't have any particular desire to be alone with each other quite yet."

"No," Laura said. "Of course not. You couldn't tell her that."

"We can go upstairs and say good-night to them. Then we can disappear quietly. Preferably through the back door."

"We can't leave without thanking your mother, Nick. That would be outrageously rude."

"Miss Finesse," he mocked gently. Still he had not taken his hand away. "Go ahead, then. See what happens."

"I will," Laura said, "if you'll let go of me."

He hesitated for a second or two and then he took his hand away. Laura smoothed her sleeve, half expecting some kind of a mark, an outline of his fingers, a singeing of the fabric. But the heliotrope faille was as perfect as it had always been.

"She's over there," Nick murmured helpfully. "Don't say I didn't warn you."

Laura took a deep breath and turned her back on him. Infuriating as it was, she found herself making an effort to walk in a straight line as she crossed the room. "Nanfran," she said, holding out her hands to the older woman. "I don't know what to say. You've done so much."

Nanfran took her hands. She wasn't a woman for indiscriminate hugs and kisses. "What?" she said. "Are you leaving already?"

"Nick thought—" Laura began.

"If I know Nicholson," Nanfran interrupted, "he thought that you should slip out the back door when no one was looking."

"I," Laura said, "have never left a party in my life without thanking my hostess. And I'm not about to start now, no matter what he says."

Nanfran laughed. "What a perfectly pigheaded young woman you are," she said. "For all that you look so prissy and fragile. Oh, you are going to be so good for him. Linda! Richard! Everyone! Nicholson and Laura are trying to slip away."

The hum of talk in the room rose abruptly to a clamor of shouts and laughter. "Shush!" someone called. "The kids are upstairs. Come on, everybody. Outside."

Laura felt a hand on her arm. She turned, expecting Nick again, and came face-to-face with his sister Linda Corey. "Surprise," Linda said. "Bet you didn't know that a Rafland isn't really married until he's been shivareed from one end of the Black Moon to the other."

"From one end to the other?" Laura repeated blankly. "What do you mean by that?"

No one answered. No one was listening. Linda was laughing, clutching her wrist, propelling her toward the front door. There was a pickup parked in the turnaround outside the house. A couple of bales of hay were stacked in the back and the tailgate had been unfastened. "Go on," Linda said. "Climb up. A shivaree always starts with a procession."

Laura stared at the truck. "You must be joking," she said. "In this skirt?"

"Allow me, Mrs. Rafland."

It was Nick, behind her. Before she could turn he took her by the waist and with no apparent effort at all he lifted her. She reached out for the side of the truck to steady herself. There was a ragged cheer.

"You, too, Nick," someone shouted.

The truck creaked and shifted, and he was standing beside her. His hair was uncharacteristically ruffled and he had a dark wild look in his eyes, part tension and part exasperation and part pure involuntary amusement. "I suppose," he said, "it would be rude for me to say 'I told you so.'"

"You didn't tell me about the pickup truck," Laura said. "I thought you meant they'd just stand under the window and bang on a few pans for a while."

"Be thankful," he said, "that we're not riding back-to-back on a donkey. That's what they used to do in— Hang on."

The truck lurched into motion. Laura staggered back against the hay bales, and Nick put his arm around her waist to steady her. The rest of the Thundering Herd trotted along beside the truck, full of hilarity and catcalls.

"The first thing," Laura said, "is to get these ridiculous high-heeled shoes off. Hold on to me."

"I am holding on to you," Nick said. "Did you have something a bit more specific in mind?"

"Oh, hush," she said brusquely. "There. Now at least I can stand up. You can let go of me now."

The truck hit a dip in the road, and they were both thrown back against the hay. The Thundering Herd cheered enthusiastically. "I think I'll just hang on to you for the time being," Nick said, close to her ear. "After going to all the trouble to marry you I don't want to lose you over the side of a truck on the very first night. Throw them the shoes."

"What?"

"Throw them the shoes. That's all part of a shivaree... appeasing the crowd by throwing them presents."

"Presents?" Laura said. "My shoes? Why on earth would anybody want my shoes?"

He laughed. "Don't be so literal," he said. "Just toss them. They'll get ruined in the lake, anyway."

"The *lake?*"

"Would you prefer the horse tank? We're going to get thrown into some kind of water somewhere, sweetheart. Another shivaree tradition."

"You can't really mean that."

"Oh, yes, I can."

He hugged her a little more closely, and for the first time Laura didn't try to pull away. In the confusion and the noise, the darkness and the dust and the precarious jolting of the truck, it was reassuring to have someone tall and hard and steady to hold on to. She braced herself against his body and flung one shoe over the side of the truck. Laughter and cheers. She had just thrown the second shoe when the truck stopped.

"Does your jacket come off?" Nick said.

"Now that," Laura said, "is going too far. The shoes, yes. But I will not throw those ravening maniacs every stitch I have on, one piece at a time."

"Those ravening maniacs," he said, "are your beloved in-laws. It's only May, Laura, and even though the weather's been warm the lake's going to be pretty cold. If you can take the jacket off and leave it here you'll have something dry to put on."

"The jacket," Laura said, "does *not* come off."

He grinned at her. His teeth were very white in his dark face. "Not ever?" he said.

"Don't be ridiculous." She slipped out of the circle of his arm. "It comes off when I choose to take it off. And I don't choose to take it off in front of the Thundering Herd."

"Fortunately for me," he said, shrugging out of his own beautifully tailored and obviously very expensive suit jacket and dropping it casually on the bales of hay, "I don't have your inhibitions."

"Fortunately for you," Laura retorted, "you have a shirt on underneath. Excuse me. I might as well get this over with."

A tall man, slighter and fairer than Nick but with the same oblique dark eyes, caught her outstretched hands and swung her down from the back of the truck. It was Richard. Or was it Michael? The lake lay before them, dark and shining and still. There was no wind and only a waning quarter of a moon. Laura felt grass and then sand under her shoeless feet.

"You're a good sport, pretty Laura," said Richard-or-Michael, laughing. "I think the ladies are calling you."

He gave her a playful little shove. The women closed in around her and the next moment she was in the water, up to her knees. Nick had been right. It was cold. Linda and Janet were splashing her, driving her deeper. Nick's brothers had dragged him down from the truck and to the edge of the lake, but he seemed to be putting up at least a token fight. Maybe that was part of the tradition, too. Up to her waist, Laura half turned. Then someone pushed her and the bottom of the lake seemed to fall away and the water closed abruptly over her head.

She gasped, and the clean cold water rushed into her mouth. She floundered a bit and broke the surface, coughing and choking. Nick's arms—and of course they were Nick's arms, although she wasn't quite sure how she knew—closed around her.

"You look like a naiad," he said. "In a ruined silk suit. They should have known better than to push you right there where the bottom drops off. Are you all right?"

"Naiad indeed," Laura sputtered, clutching at his arms. "How poetic. You just look wet. Hold on to me."

"I am holding on to you."

"Wet, and neat. You have to be the only man in the world, Nick Rafland, who can be pushed in a lake and look neat at the same time. If you let go of me I'm going to *strangle* you."

He laughed. "I'm not going to let go of you," he said. "My lovely water-maiden."

"I'm not your lovely water-maiden," she said. "I'm not your lovely water-anything."

He brushed a wet strand of her hair out of her eyes. "Oh, yes, you are," he said. "You're my lovely water-wife."

Her face was as cold and as wet as the rest of her, and his cheek against hers was surprisingly warm. She clung to him and tried to reach the bottom with her toes and after a moment she turned her head and...

His lips were soft at first, very gentle. Little kisses, light, questioning, with tiny breathless pauses in between. Sweet hot confounding pleasure coursed through her.

He made a sound, inarticulate. His mouth moved, parting her lips, tasting her, a deliberate unmistakable possession. Laura's legs trembled, and for a few seconds that seemed like forever the pleasure was strong enough. But then the dark and the cold and the sickness rose up again and blotted it out.

He must have felt her abrupt panicky withdrawal, because he lifted his head. "Shh," he murmured. His lips just brushed the thin sensitive skin at the corner of her eye. "It's all right, Laura. It's only me."

Nick. It was Nick. And somehow she knew that she was safe, after all. She struggled to catch her breath, to get away from him and stand up on her own.

He drew her a few more steps toward the shore and let her go, all but one steadying hand on her waist. "Amazon," he murmured. "I'm sorry about your suit. I'll get you another one just like it."

The suit. The suit. Something else to think about. Something else to talk about...

"Don't you dare," Laura gasped. "I'm glad it's ruined. Even before I came downstairs this afternoon I was thinking that I never wanted to see it again."

"The suit you were married in? How unsentimental you are."

"A kiss or two," she said, still breathless, "is hardly going to make me sentimental about getting married. Can we get out of the lake now? Your lovely water-wife's lovely water-teeth are starting to chatter."

"I think we're both wet and cold enough to satisfy everybody," he said. "Here, let me—"

"I can walk by myself, thank you," she said. "Well, wade by myself. Leave me alone."

The procession's next stop was Nick's house. Still not content to just stand under the windows and bang on pans, the Thundering Herd followed them up onto the veranda, through the front door and up the stairs. Followed them...

"Nick!" Laura called frantically, struggling to make herself heard above the din. "For heaven's sake! Are they going to come right into our bedrooms?"

No one seemed to notice the plural. The swarm pressed around them, shrieking with laughter. Then they were in a room and the door had slammed shut behind them. Nick turned immediately, and Laura heard him wrench at the knob, one way and then the other.

The door was immovable.

"Hell," he said through his teeth. "They've locked us in."

He turned again and stood with his back to the door, looking at her. Laura stared back, exasperated, shivering, clutching his jacket over the devastated remains of her wedding suit.

For a long moment neither one of them moved.

"Well," he said at last, "at the risk of sounding like the villain in a very bad movie, I think you might want to get out of those wet clothes."

"In case you haven't noticed," Laura said, "we've been locked in your bedroom. My room is going to be at the other end of the hall. All my things are there. If I get out of these wet clothes here, what exactly are you proposing I get into?"

Under the windows the clashing and pounding and ringing had started at last. One corner of Nick's mouth twitched very faintly, that clear-cut sensual mouth that could tighten into such a hard purposeful line, soften into sudden unexpected sensitivity, curve into the most ironic and self-mocking of smiles. "There are drawers full of shirts and sweaters and pajamas," he said mildly. "A couple of robes in the closet. Sweats. Jeans. Suits and ties, for that matter, if wearing my jacket has given you a taste for the tailored look. Pick anything you like."

She looked at him for a moment. And then a little unwillingly she smiled back. "I'm overreacting, aren't I?" she said.

"Just a bit," he said. "But you've had a stressful day."

"A stressful six weeks," Laura said, "is more like it. And now that it's over, all I want to do..." Out of nowhere an enormous yawn rose in her throat. She pressed her hands against her mouth and shook her head slightly. "All I want to do," she repeated, "is to get dry and get warm and go to *bed.*"

"What a charming suggestion, Mrs. Rafland."

"It wasn't meant to be a suggestion," she said. "Charming or otherwise. I wish you wouldn't do that, Nick."

"Do what?"

"Tease me."

"Am I teasing you?"

"You'd better be. You promised."

"*You promised,*" he mocked softly. "You sound like Becky when she wants me to take her to McDonald's. Are you going to change your clothes or are you going to stand there and shiver all night?"

"I'm going to change," she said.

"That door is the bathroom," he said. "The closets are on either side as you go in. Take a hot shower while you're at it and get yourself warm."

"I will," she said. "A very hot shower. If I can stay awake long enough I may use all the hot water for miles around. Since the lake didn't seem to do it, a nice cold shower might be just the thing to subdue your nuptial ardor. *Mr.* Rafland."

He started to laugh. She took off his jacket and dropped it on the floor as if it were infected with some virulently loathsome disease. Then she turned and stalked into the bathroom.

The hot water and the dry fleecy warmth of one of Nick's sweatshirts were more soporific than the strongest sleeping pill. Laura had to struggle to keep her eyes open long enough to drag on the pants that went with the shirt and to pull the drawstring for what seemed like forever until she was sure the pants were secure around her waist. Then she had to roll the legs up around her ankles to keep from tripping over them.

When she finally came out of the bathroom the bed had been neatly turned down. Nick himself had changed into faded old jeans and a russet-brown shirt. He was ensconced in the depths of a comfortable-looking leather chair next to the window.

The shivaree had apparently turned into a modern-day party on the veranda. The pans and bells had been abandoned and the raucous thudding beat of rock music had taken their place.

"One unoccupied bed," Nick said, gesturing casually. "As requested. And from the look of you, not a moment too soon."

"What are you going to do?" Laura demanded. The bed looked so inviting. The green-and-black comforter looked so thick and soft. The sheets looked so white and crisp and fresh. "Sleep in that chair, I hope."

"I don't know if I'm going to sleep at all if this noise goes on," he said. "If you collapse where you stand, Laura, I'm going to pick you up and put you to bed myself, and there's no telling where that might lead."

"All right," Laura mumbled. "All *right*. Leave me alone." She walked around the bed and let herself sink down on the side that had been turned back. The sheets were crisp and fresh indeed, and so lovely to touch. Against her cheek, the pillowcase was...

Suddenly she jerked awake. It seemed as if only a mo-
ient had passed. At first she thought she was back in her
wn bedroom in the cottage on Tenth Street, but the feel of
ue bed wasn't right. The scent of the sheets wasn't right. It
as dark and silent, and for some reason the silence seemed
rong, too.

And she wasn't alone.

"Who's there?" she said sharply, into the blackness.

Leather creaked, somewhere on the other side of the
oom. Then a hand touched her shoulder. Laura started vi-
lently.

"Shh. It's only me."

Nick Rafland's voice. Disoriented as she was, she recog-
ized it instantly. What on earth . . .?

"Nick," she said. "What are you doing here?"

He laughed softly, hardly more than a breath. The bed
hifted as he sat down beside her. "I live here," he said.
And so do you, now. On weekends, at least. Don't tell me
ou've forgotten already."

"Oh," she said blankly. A little at a time she relaxed back
ito the pillows. "This is the ranch house. This is your
oom. We're *married.*"

"So we are," he said. "You don't sound very happy
bout it."

"What happened to the shivaree?"

"By two o'clock or so they couldn't stand their own noise
nymore. They're gone."

"Did they unlock the door?"

He reached out and skimmed his fingertips very lightly
cross her forehead, drawing a loose strand of her hair back
om her face. "No," he said. "But don't worry. They'll be
ack in the morning to let us out. With suitable witticisms,
f course."

"I can hardly wait," Laura muttered. Deliberately she
hook her head so that the hair fell across her eyes again. "I
hink I'd almost rather be locked in here forever."

"I can think of worse places to be. Go back to sleep."

She slid down among the pillows. "Go back to your chair," she countered.

"In a minute." He picked up her left hand and thoughtfully fingered the circle of the platinum wedding band half hidden under the moonstone. "Are you sorry?"

She tried to tug her hand away. "Sorry about what?"

For the first time he didn't let her go at the slightest hint of resistance. "Don't be obtuse," he said. "Tell me."

"It's a good thing you didn't ask me that a few hours ago," Laura said perversely. "About the time they chased us up the stairs I was as sorry as I could be."

He smiled. She couldn't see it so much as she could hear it in the sound of his words. "I can hardly blame you," he said. "But that was a few hours ago. What about now?"

After a moment she stopped trying to free her hand. The truth was that it was surprisingly pleasant to lie curled there, only half awake, wrapped in clean-smelling sheets and a thick soft down-filled comforter, with Nick Rafland's steady hard-muscled weight beside her in the dark and Nick Rafland's hand holding hers. He had strong hands. Gentle hands. Somewhere she had seen him do something, make some gesture, strong hands, gentle hands, two small silky heads and a circle of light....

She closed her eyes.

"Laura?" he said softly. "Tell me. Are you sorry?"

"No," she murmured. "Not 'ny more."

He didn't let go of her. He didn't get up and go back to his chair. But it didn't seem to matter so much anymore. He sat there beside her, saying nothing. He might even have lifted her hand and kissed her fingertips very lightly. But the line between what was real and what was a dream was beginning to blur. Laura let her hand rest in his, and slept.

Chapter Seven

Sunlight on her face woke her again at last, and this time aura knew where she was even before she opened her eyes. he ranch house. Nick's room. Nick's bed, of all places. Vithout thinking she reached out drowsily for something at should have been there.

Her hand closed on emptiness.

Laura sat up suddenly.

The curtains were open and the room was flooded with ght. Nick was gone. The door was slightly but definitely jar.

"Oh, you rat," she said aloud. "You treacherous black-aired black-hearted fibbing *rat.* It was open all along."

She slipped out of the bed and went to the door. The allway was as empty as the bedroom was. But the rich tan-alizing scent of coffee was floating up from somewhere ownstairs. And the door to her own room down the hall as open as well.

"Just you give me a minute to get dressed in my own othes," she said ominously. "I can't believe that I let you get away with it. I can't believe that I let you sit there an hold my hand and..." She could feel the heat of a flus rising in her cheeks and throat. "Oh, you just wait. You jus wait."

In her own bedroom she stripped off Nick's sweatshir and pants and pulled on her own jeans, her own favorit white shirt and the purple suede vest for luck. Vigorousl she brushed her hair back from her face and clipped it wit her tortoise-shell barrette. Now, she thought, for some o that coffee. Coffee and breakfast and a piece of my mind fo my brand-new husband.

Her brand-new husband was sitting on the veranda, tilte back in his chair, with his long legs stretched out in front o him and his booted heels resting comfortably on the plank and-post railing. His strong bony hands were cupped loosel around a mug of coffee, and he was gazing off to the nort with a remote considering look on his face. All of a sud den, as if he sensed her standing there, he turned his head.

"Good morning," he said. "There's coffee in the kit chen."

Laura held up her own cup. "I found it," she said. "Th door was never locked at all, was it?"

Nick raised his eyebrows. His surprise seemed genuine "The bedroom door?" he said. "Yes, it was."

"Then how did you get out?"

He grinned at her suddenly. Her heart, traitor that it was faltered in its rhythm. "Why, Mrs. Rafland," he said "Married less than a day, and already you think I'm de ceiving you."

"Well, are you?" she demanded warily. "Last night w were locked in. This morning I wake up to find the doo standing open and you sitting out here with your feet u drinking coffee as if you don't have a care in the world."

He laughed. "Richard slipped over early this mornin and opened the door," he said. "He seems to have con ceived a liking for you, and he said he wanted to spare yo the final indignities. I didn't wake you because after you rather boisterous night I thought you might want all the sleep you could get."

"Oh," Laura said stiffly. "I see. Richard."

"Yes," he said. "Richard. I swear. So take the starch out of your spine, my lovely new wife, and sit down. We should have at least a few more minutes of connubial peace to drink our coffee before Emmie and Becky descend upon us."

She didn't sit down. Instead she leaned against one of the veranda posts and looked out to the north, where he had been looking. It was where the land was, the land he wanted, the original site of the Black Moon homestead. Eleanor Kinnard's land.

"I'm sorry," she said after a moment. "About not believing you, I mean." She tasted her coffee. "Nick?"

"Hmm?"

"I'm sorry about last night, too. Out at the lake. I'm not being very consistent, am I?"

"I seem to have lived through it," he said dryly. There was a pause. Then, in a different voice, he said, "When are you going to tell me about it?"

"About what?"

"About why you don't want to be touched. Why you're afraid to be touched."

She looked down at her coffee. "I'm not afraid," she said.

"You don't really expect me to believe that."

"I'm not afraid of you, at least."

"Considering the rather unconventional way you and I first met, I'm glad to hear it. Who are you afraid of, sweetheart?"

The unexpected endearment made Laura's view of her coffee cup blur for just a second or two. She blinked. "Nobody," she said. "Nobody real, not anymore."

"It had to start somewhere. With someone."

"Oh, Nick. Does it matter?"

"The longer you keep trying to hide it away, the longer it's going to take you to leave it behind."

He was right, of course. "And I have to leave it behind," she said, with sudden perverse contentiousness, "at all costs. Right? The sooner, the better."

"I have to admit," he said, "that it was an unanticipated temptation to watch you sleeping in my bed last night."

She swung around to face him. "Don't be ridiculous. My hair was all in wet strings and my makeup was washed off in the lake and I was wearing one of your old sweat suits."

He smiled at her. "I repeat," he said. "An unanticipated temptation."

"You must be very easily tempted," she said. "The girls are coming. Walking over from Nanfran's."

Nick swung his feet down from the rail and let his chair drop forward so that it rested more conventionally on all four of its legs. "And so our little family circle," he said, "is about to be complete. Good morning, Emmie, sweetheart. Good morning, Becky. Did you have fun sleeping over at Nanfran's with your cousins?"

"Oh, yes," Becky said. "We got to pop popcorn and stay up late and we heard all the yelling and everything. Did you and Miss Finesse have fun, too, sleeping over here all by yourselves?"

The coffee mug almost slipped out of Laura's hands. She clutched at it precariously. The coffee splashed over her fingers.

"Yes," Nick said gravely. There was only the very faintest tremor at one corner of his mouth. "We did have fun. Once the . . . yelling was over. Did you burn yourself, Laura?"

"No," Laura said. "I'm fine."

Emily hesitated at the bottom of the veranda steps. "Can I ask you a question about you being married?" she said in her soft serious voice. "An *important* question?"

"Sure," Nick said easily. "Come sit for a minute before we go in and have breakfast. You, too, Laura." He smiled up at her. "Sit down. You look as if you're about to swoon away."

"I'm no more about to swoon away than you are," Laura retorted. She put her coffee mug on the table and seated herself with as much dignity as she could muster. "Come on, Emily, sit by me. What's your question?"

Becky ran up the stairs and plumped happily into the chair next to Nick. Emily went to her own chair a little more slowly, and perched tensely on the very edge of the seat. She reached out and slipped her hand into Laura's. "You and Uncle Nick are really married now, aren't you?" she said.

"Yes," Laura said firmly. "We're really married."

"Of *course* they're married," Becky said. "I told you, silly. The thing with the judge and all that stuff is only part of it. It's what happens *afterward* that makes them really married."

Utter silence descended. Even Nick looked a little nonplussed. Becky glanced around the table triumphantly. "It's the shivering that does it," she said. "We heard Aunt Linda talking to Aunt Janet about it. Everybody makes a lot of noise and they throw you in the lake and keep you there until you get cold and when you're shivering they let you out and then you're really married."

Nick leaned back in his chair again and started to laugh. Laura herself couldn't keep from smiling. She squeezed Emily's hand affectionately. "What your Aunt Linda was talking about," she said, "is a 'shivaree.' That's what people call all the noise and the celebration and the... silly practical jokes they play after a wedding. After some weddings, anyway. It sounds a lot like 'shivering' but it's a different word."

"Although your brand-new Aunt Laura," Nick put in, "was certainly shivering from head to toe when I pulled her out of the lake last night. Shivering rather charmingly, I might add."

"You did not pull me out of the lake," Laura said. "I got out all by myself."

"All I really wanted to *ask*," Emily said, a little plaintively, "is if that's what we're supposed to call you now.

Aunt Laura. Jimmy and Courtney and Derek said that if you're married to Uncle Nick, you have to be Aunt Laura. But Becky says she doesn't want you to be."

"She doesn't?" Laura turned and looked at Becky. The little girl's silky brows drew together in a frown that was absurdly like Nick's own. "Why not, honey?" Laura said gently.

"Because," Becky said.

"Do you want to keep calling me Miss Finesse?"

"No."

"What do you want to call me, then?"

Becky glowered and said nothing.

"If she's not an aunt," Emily argued tremulously, "she's not even really *related.* There isn't anything to keep her from going away like..." She stopped. Her hand clutched at Laura's. *Like* she *did,* her dark anxious eyes said. *That other Miss Finesse. The one that neither one of us can remember. Or even like Daddy did...*

"But we've already got a whole lot of aunts," Becky burst out. "I don't want her to be related like an aunt. I want her to be special. And I hate Jimmy and Courtney and Derek anyway. They always think they know everything."

"Wait a minute," Nick said. He leaned forward, his dark eyes somber and his soft deep voice suddenly and intensely serious. "Both of you. In the first place, I don't want to hear about anybody hating anybody, Rebecca Marie. In the second place, Laura and I are married, really, truly, once and for all, and for good. I am your uncle and so she is your aunt. She is related to all of us now, and she's not going to go away. Do you understand?"

Both girls nodded wordlessly. Caught by his certainty, Laura realized that she was nodding, too. Believing him. Trusting him. *Really, truly, once and for all, and for good...*

"Now," he went on. A spark of humor had come back into his eyes. "You can call her anything you like. Miss Laura or Aunt Laura or Miss Finesse. Laura, do you have a preference?"

"No," Laura said. She squeezed Emily's hand again. "You just call me whatever you want, honey. Whatever you both want."

"Aunt Laura," Emily whispered. "So you match Uncle Nick."

"Becky?"

"I want to call you Mom," Becky said defiantly. "Emily can call you Aunt Laura if she wants to, but I want to call you Mom."

Laura swallowed hard. "I'm not really your mother, honey," she said. "You know that. And anyway, I—"

"I don't care. You can make believe, can't you? I do. I make believe you're my mom all the time. Sometimes I even forget it's not really real. If you make believe, maybe you'll forget, too."

"Grownups aren't very good at make-believe," Laura said. "But I'll try. I promise I'll try." Her throat felt so tight that it was a little hard to get the words out clearly. "And remember? I always... always... *always* keep my promises."

"You're a sly fox, Nick Rafland," Eleanor Kinnard said. She drank the last of her champagne with a flourish. "Planning to get married all along and never breathing a word of it to me. Or did you just go out and recruit this young lady to play the part of your wife to bamboozle me into keeping my promise?"

"Laura is hardly playing the part of my wife," Nick said. "Our marriage is perfectly genuine. Would you like more wine?"

Although I might as well be playing a part, Laura thought. He's not interested in Laura-on-the-inside tonight. He just wants Miss Finesse to sit here and wear his antique moonstone ring and be genuinely married to him, amid the white damask tablecloths and the fresh flowers and the four forks at every place.

Am I a make-believe wife as well as a make-believe mom?

Why does it seem to matter, all of a sudden?

"Just a teeny sip," Eleanor Kinnard was saying. "I have to keep my wits about me when I'm sitting across the table from a Rafland. You're all a pack of scoundrels. And you, Nick Rafland, you're no better than your Uncle Jack was."

"Great-uncle," Nick said calmly. "Why do you say that?"

"Oh, I don't know." Eleanor shrugged and smiled. The enormous diamonds in her ears sparkled in the soft four-fork-restaurant light. "You just have that dark scoundrelly look about you."

Nick smiled back at her. He hadn't made any visible gesture but all of a sudden the wine waiter was at his elbow, bowing, taking the bottle of Pouilly-Foussé from the silver cooler, wrapping it deftly in a fresh napkin and refilling the glasses. "My wife," he said, "would be the best judge of that, I think. Do I have a dark scoundrelly look about me, Laura?"

"Of course not," Laura said politely.

"Well, scoundrel or not," Eleanor said, "I certainly didn't expect you to take me seriously when I told you to go out and find yourself a wife. Now what am I going to do?"

"The answer to that," Nick said, "would seem to be obvious. You're going to keep your promise and sell me back the land that's the heart of the Black Moon. I'm perfectly willing to—"

"The heart?" Eleanor interrupted archly. "Why, Nick. How very romantic. Marriage must agree with you." She turned suddenly and looked at Laura. "Perhaps I should sell the land to your charming new wife instead."

For a moment no one said anything. Eleanor Kinnard's eyes glittered under her wrinkled eyelids, bright and icy as her diamonds. Nick's dark face showed no surprise and only the mildest of interest.

"Sell it to me?" Laura repeated lightly. "I think that's a marvelous idea. I'm sure we could—"

"Absolutely not," Eleanor said. She seemed to enjoy her own inconsistency as much as she enjoyed the deliberate rudeness of her interruptions. "That would be too easy. And anyway, just because I said I'd sell it to Nick here if he got married doesn't mean that I can't change my mind. So if the land is the only reason why you two got married in such a hurry, you now have my permission to repent at leisure."

"I don't feel particularly repentant," Nick said easily. "Do you, Laura?"

Yes, Laura thought. *No. Sometimes. I don't know....*

"No," she said. After all, he didn't really want an honest answer. "Not at all."

Eleanor frowned. "I didn't say that I *was* going to change my mind," she said. "Just that I could if I wanted to. Well, if you didn't get married just to call my bluff, then I suppose you, Nick, were looking for a housekeeper and a nursemaid. You must need one now that you have Kit's girls."

Under the table Laura clenched her fists in her napkin. Why, you barefaced old witch, she thought. How dare you?

"I was looking—" Nick began.

Laura looked at him, and he stopped.

"Housekeeping," she said to Eleanor Kinnard with perfect truthfulness, "is not one of the things Nick and I discussed when we decided to get married. And Emily and Becky don't need a nursemaid. They have beautiful manners."

"I doubt that," Eleanor said airily. "Considering the way they've been brought up, with no mother and Kit Rafland for a father and a scoundrel for an uncle. But I'll give you credit, Laura Rafland, for sticking up for them. For sticking up for yourself, too. You're presentable enough as a wife for Nick here, I suppose, even if you can't hold a candle to Julie McAllister."

Nick was taking a sip of the champagne. His hand holding the fragile crystal tulip glass remained perfectly steady and his equable self-contained expression didn't change.

There was nothing at all to support Laura's sudden unnerving impression that he had recoiled as if Eleanor Kinnard had struck him a physical blow.

He put down the glass. For a few seconds he simply looked at it. Then he looked up again. There was a stillness that Laura had never seen before in his oblique dark eyes.

"How very odd that you should say such a thing," he said. "The truth is that I've been thinking just the opposite."

He held out his right hand. Not quite sure of his intention, Laura let go of her crumpled napkin and put her left hand in his. The moonstone caught the light with a soft opaline glimmer that was utterly unlike the icy flash of Eleanor Kinnard's diamonds.

"But then I shouldn't have to explain to you, Eleanor, of all people, how I feel about Laura," he went on softly. "After all, I did marry her, didn't I?"

Laura stopped breathing. Jack Rafland, all those years ago, had refused to marry Eleanor Kinnard. And that was what had started the whole bitter rivalry over the land....

Unexpectedly, a little shrilly, Eleanor laughed. "You like to live dangerously, don't you, Nick Rafland?" she said.

He continued to hold Laura's hand in his. "Not as dangerously as you do," he said.

"All right," Eleanor said. "You win. This time." She turned to Laura. "Laura, my dear, I do beg your pardon. That was an inexcusable remark."

"Yes," Laura said. "It was. Thank you for apologizing. We won't have to discuss it any further, then."

"And just to show you that I mean what I say, I'll ask my lawyers to start drawing up the paperwork on that piece of land your husband is so bound and determined to have. But that doesn't mean I can't change my mind again. And it doesn't mean I won't make him pay a perfectly unconscionable price."

"I think," Laura murmured, "you already have."

She tried to draw her hand away from Nick's. For just a moment his long fingers closed around hers. She could feel the moonstone and the platinum wedding ring pressing against her skin. Not hard enough to hurt. Just hard enough to remind her that they were there.

Then he let her go.

The truth is that I've been thinking just the opposite.

But of course it was nothing more than a calculated move in his intricate game with Eleanor Kinnard.

Of course he didn't really mean it.

The purple cushions, Nick thought as he closed the front door behind him, had been a little jarring at first in the town house's symmetrical flax-colored living room. But after three wary weeks of marriage to Laura he was getting used to them. More than that. He was actually beginning to like them. He walked through the living room and down the hall, past his own bedroom. Her door was open. Her light was on.

"Laura?" he said softly.

There was no answer. The room was empty.

He walked back down the hall. The glass doors were unlatched, and he could see just a glimmer of her hair, spread out over the arm of the chaise. Very quietly he went out onto the deck.

She was asleep. A yellow legal pad, the top sheet half covered with her precise round handwriting, lay next to her. He crouched down beside the chaise and reached out to smooth the ruffled light brown silk of her hair away from her cheek. The moon was full and the leaves of the lemon trees cast a faint shifting pattern of light and shadow over her face and throat. She looked so far away in her sleep, so mysterious and so fragile, that for a moment it was a little hard to breathe.

Mine, he thought.

Mine?

He drew back, surprised at himself. It wasn't love, of course. It couldn't be love. It was something entirely new, something he'd never felt before. There was tenderness in it. There was admiration and appreciation and warmth. But there was something else, too, an elemental bone-deep possessiveness, a fierce visceral gratification that this particular woman lived in his house and bore his name and wore a generations-old moonstone-and-amethyst ring on her slender finger.

Is there that much of a Stone Age barbarian, he wondered, lurking under my ostensibly civilized twentieth-century skin? Apparently there is. Right now I feel as if I could kill any other man who ever dared to touch her. Any person who ever dared to hurt her or frighten her, the way that contemptible fool of a boy apparently did, all those years ago. The way Eleanor Kinnard did the other night at dinner. And I'm not sure that I like confronting myself in quite that light.

After all, she sees me as... what did she say? *A working rancher and the guardian of two little girls and a hawk among the dovecotes of the Austin society hostesses and a spectacularly successful entrepreneur into the bargain.* Not to mention Don Quixote tilting at windmills, for God's sake. I like that better than Stone Age barbarian. Oh, yes, I like that a lot better.

She opened her eyes.

"Oh," she said. "Nick. I was just working on next Monday's column, and then I... What time is it?"

"The stroke of midnight," he said. "What are you writing about, Cinderella?"

She sat up and reached for the legal pad. She tore off the top sheet and folded it in half. "Nothing," she said.

"If it's going to run in Monday's *Times* you can hardly keep it a secret."

"This isn't the column. I finished that. It's... well, it's a letter to Edward Fournier. The lawyer in Charleston. Telling him that I'm married."

Nick sat back on his heels and looked at her. "Are you just getting around to writing that?" he said. "I would have thought you'd have done it right away."

"I started to," she said. "A hundred times. But I just couldn't finish it."

"Why not?"

"Oh, Nick," she said. "Now that I can just write to Edward Fournier and ask for that letter I don't know if I want it anymore. I don't know if I want to find out who my father was. Aunt Grace never told me, after all. She always said... Maybe there was a reason why she didn't tell me."

Her hands were trembling, crumpling the piece of yellow paper. He reached out and took them between his own and steadied them. She didn't try to pull away. At least, he thought wryly, we've progressed to the point where handholding is tolerable.

"What did she always say?" he said gently.

"Actually it was about me, not him. She always said that I was born with a hedonistic and disorderly nature. Hedonistic and disorderly. The same words, every time. I didn't even know what it meant at first. I thought it was one long grown-up word, hedonistic-and-disorderly. But she said I was born with it, you see. Born with it."

"And since your Aunt Grace herself was apparently anything but hedonistic and disorderly, she must have meant that it came from your father."

"Yes. Yes. Nick, maybe it would be better if I just never—"

"Sensuous," he said suddenly.

"What?"

"And spontaneous. Pleasure-loving and creative."

"What in heaven's name are you *talking* about?"

"Hedonistic, sensuous, pleasure-loving. Disorderly, spontaneous, creative. They could all be just different ways of saying the same thing, Laura."

She stared at him. The moonlight was bright enough for him to see the trace of violet in her eyes. His desire to touch her hair again, her face, her skin, now that she was awake and aware of his presence, was so strong that it threatened to overwhelm him. He stood up suddenly and walked to the other side of the deck.

"Nick?" she said uncertainly.

Sensuous. Pleasure-loving. Spontaneous...

He looked at the lake. His mouth was dry and his hands were unsteady and his own flesh, always so disciplined, was betraying him. "It's all right," he said automatically. "Don't be afraid, Laura. You know you really want to know."

"But what about the weakness that runs in his family?" she said. "What if it wasn't just one of her old-fashioned notions? What if there's...well, something wrong with me?"

"There's nothing wrong with you."

"But I can't be sure."

"There's only one way to be sure. Finish your letter to the lawyer. Send it. Get your Aunt Grace's original letter and read it. That is why you married me, isn't it?"

A small hesitation. "That's one reason," she said.

"And the girls," he said, still without turning to look at her, "are the other. I know. That's why I wanted to talk to you, in fact. I finally heard from Sharon Scott today."

"You did?" A rustling sound. He could see her as clearly as if he were facing her, sitting bolt upright, shaking back her hair, dropping the folded and crumpled piece of yellow paper. Any hint of a threat to Emmie and Becky, he thought, and she forgets everything else in the world. "What did she say?"

"She didn't talk to me personally. She talked to Mike Lyle. One of my attorneys. She wants money."

"Money? What do you mean, money? Money for what?"

At last his hands were steady again. It felt safe to turn. He did. "Two hundred thousand dollars," he said. "For signing the papers, of course."

"Two hundred thousand dollars?" she said. "For signing... But that's...that's...that's outrageous. That's despicable. For God's sake, Nick, is that even *legal?*"

"Not as a direct transaction," he said dryly. "But there are ways around that. There are always ways."

"She wants to *sell* them. Her own girls. *Our* girls. Emily and Becky. That's unnatural. That's *immoral.* Nick, you're not going to pay her, are you?"

"Of course not," he said. "Mike's filing a custody suit in California, and a motion to try to get the case transferred back here. But it looks as if it may be an ugly battle after all."

"I don't care," Laura said. "She's...she's...she's nothing but a windmill. A greedy cold-blooded windmill. We'll fight her together, Don Quixote."

She stood up and walked toward him, and with his back to the rail of the deck there was no way he could retreat any further. When she was close enough for him to feel the warmth of her body she reached out and put her hand on his arm. It was the first time she had touched him entirely of her own volition.

"That is why you married me, isn't it?" she said.

Under her touch, through his jacket and his shirtsleeve, a small hand-shaped patch of his skin began to feel painfully sensitive, as if it had never been touched before.

"That's one reason," he said.

Chapter Eight

Grace Gardiner's rosewood dressing table was the one vestige of her old life in her new bedroom at Nick Rafland's town house. Laura was sitting in front of the mirror brushing her hair when footsteps came pattering down the hall. A sudden double fusillade of knocks sounded, halfway down the bedroom door. She smiled at herself in the mirror.

"Come in," she said.

Becky burst into the room with Emily on her heels. She was clutching a white box. "Look, Mom," she said breathlessly. "We have a present for you, 'cause you're going to a big chair. . . chair. . . chair-something."

"Charity," Emily put in. "A charity ball."

"A ball. Like Cinderella. And this is a present from us. Well, it's from Uncle Nick, really, but he said we could give it to you. It's flowers."

"You weren't supposed to *tell* her," Emily said. "It was supposed to be a surprise."

Becky put the box in Laura's hands. "Open it," she said. "Quick. I want to see."

"We'll all see together," Laura said. "Come on, Emily."

The girls pressed against her on either side, and she opened the box. Not an orchid. Not a cluster of tight little rosebuds impaled with a pearl-headed pin. Not a corsage or a nosegay at all. Just a small bunch of white violets, fresh and cool, their long damp stems tied loosely and very simply with a narrow purple ribbon. Fresh violets. In Austin. In July. There was no card.

"Oh," Becky said. She sounded disappointed. "I thought they'd be bigger."

"Are you going to wear them?" Emily said. "Look, they're purple in the middle. They'd go with your dress."

"They're beautiful," Laura said. "Thank you. Both of you. No, I don't think I'll try to wear them. They're too fragile, and I want to keep them as long as I can. What I really need is a little vase with some water in it."

"I'll get it," Emily said.

"No, I will," Becky said.

They ran out of the room together. Laura smiled again, put the box down on the dressing table and turned back to the mirror. There in the glass, standing in the doorway behind her, she saw Nick himself.

He smiled at her. "You really do have to tell me," he said, "the difference between a mother and a mom. Whichever you are, you're certainly being outstandingly successful at it. May I come in?"

He was obviously a member of the strictly traditional black-and-white school of thought on evening dress for gentlemen. His black dinner jacket was severely cut. His shirt was white, the collar stiffly starched and the dull black silk cravat precisely knotted. Somehow all the immaculate formality only heightened the elemental physical shape of his body, his height, the length of his legs, the latent power of his arms and shoulders.

"Of course you can come in," Laura said. "A mother is just more... well, more serious, I guess, that's all. A mom sounds so offhand. So casual. It's hard for me to think of myself as a mom."

"It was hard for you to think of yourself as sensuous and spontaneous, too," he said slowly. "Instead of hedonistic and disorderly. Did you send for your letter, by the way?"

"Yes," Laura said briefly. She stood up. "I'm almost ready. Do you like my dress?"

She turned slowly. The dress was made of silk chiffon, its skirt layered in floating handkerchief-pointed petals, all in shades of violet from the palest silvery lilac to the velvety purple-black of pansies. The bodice was cut in graceful low V-shapes front and back.

"I like it very much," he said. "Somehow I knew you'd be wearing something purple. Sit down again, Mrs. Rafland. I have a present I'd like to give you."

She sank back into the chair. "The girls already gave me the flowers," she said. "Thank you."

"They reminded me of you," he said. "That's all." He put his hands very lightly on her bare shoulders and turned her to face the mirror again. Their eyes met in the glass. "But I'm not talking about the flowers now. When I gave you your ring, I think I told you that there was something else I would give you someday. And I thought tonight might be the perfect moment."

His hands felt warm and his fingers looked tanned and vital against her skin. Uneasiness trembled in Laura's stomach. And it was perfectly ridiculous to feel that way, of course. This is Nick, she thought. Nick, who has always been so calm and kind and steady. Nick, who's been my husband now for almost two months.

Two months. Two months. Her own voice: *Can we wait a little while?*

How long, exactly, was a little while?

Her uneasiness grew, the familiar mixture of sickness and apprehension. And yet as there had always been with Nick there was another element in it, too, something falteringly, tentatively expectant that was a little frightening in itself. And tonight the Nick-feeling was almost as strong as the other. Laura had to clench her teeth and force herself to sit quietly under his touch.

He lifted his hands. "Well, maybe not the perfect moment, after all," he said. There was the very faintest flicker of self-mockery at one corner of his mouth. "But I want you to have it anyway. And that dress might have been made to wear with it."

He took a flat oblong case out of his jacket pocket. It was covered with violet moiré silk. He opened it and put it down on the dressing table in front of her.

The necklace was unmistakably a companion piece to the ring, a chain of milky oval moonstones encircled with cabochon amethysts. The platinum settings and the links between the stones were worn thin with age. Somehow it managed to look sumptuous and very simple all at once. Laura drew in her breath.

"Oh, Nick," she said. "It's magnificent. But I can't wear it. Good heavens, it should be in a museum or something."

"I don't think so," he said. He picked up the necklace by the two halves of its delicate old-fashioned clasp, and for a moment it hung suspended between his hands in a shimmering opalescent-violet crescent. Then he lifted it over her head and brought it to rest very gently against her throat.

"Lift your hair," he said.

She bent her head and caught her hair up in her hands. He fastened the clasp of the necklace without touching her skin again. Then he stepped back. She let her hair fall and looked up.

"Nick," she said hesitantly. "Listen. There's something different—"

"I have the water, Aunt Laura," Emily called from the hallway.

"She spilled a lot of it," Becky said.

"Only because you joggled me."

"I wanted to carry it."

"You carried the box with the flowers."

Becky's brows drew together alarmingly. "I don't *care,*" she said. "*I* wanted to give them to her."

"Settle down, you two," Nick said. "Your Aunt Laura is about to have her first experience among the...dovecotes of the Austin society hostesses, and the last thing she needs right now is to end up in the middle of a combat zone."

"Don't scold them," Laura said. "They're just excited. Put the water here, honey."

Emily put the water on the dressing table. It was an ordinary drinking glass, and despite its joggling in the hallway it was still almost full. "Are there really going to be doves at the ball?" she said. "With coats? In the summer?"

Nick laughed. The tension in his eyes and mouth had disappeared. Almost disappeared. "No, my sweetheart," he said. "No doves, not really. And not that kind of coats, either. Come on, let's go downstairs so your Aunt Laura can finish getting ready."

When they were gone Laura untied the ribbon around the violets' crisp threadlike stems and picked them up. Their scent was pure and sweet and heady, at once innocent and sensual. *They reminded me of you....* After a moment she put them into the glass and looked up at the mirror again.

Her eyes looked bigger, darker, a little wary. Her hair was still ruffled in the back where she had gathered it up to allow him to fasten the clasp of the necklace. The opulent old-fashioned moonstones and amethysts made her look like a different person. Older. More elegant. More a lady. No. More a woman.

The necklace. Femininity. The violets. Exquisite artless sensuality. Nick's image in the mirror, his fingers lean and brown against the whiteness of her shoulders. *The perfect moment...*

Uneasiness stirred again, and the familiar bitter taste rose in Laura's throat. The old bitter taste. The bitter taste, perhaps, that had lived far beyond its proper place and time.

She swallowed hard. Then she took a deep breath and picked up her hairbrush.

"Excuse me, Mrs. Rafland." The bellman at her elbow was unobtrusive, quietly deferential. "There is a telephone call for you in the concierge's office. The young lady on the phone sounds... distraught."

"Distraught?" Automatically Laura turned around and looked for Nick. She had been talking to some of her newspaper friends and he had been talking to a man about breeding Charolais cattle and somehow in the press of people he had disappeared. She turned again and followed the bellman to the edge of the ballroom. "What's the matter?" she said.

"I don't know, madam. She simply asked for you."

There was only one young lady who could possibly be calling the Hyatt and asking for Mrs. Rafland: the girl who was taking care of Emily and Becky. Linda Corey's fifteen-year-old, Nancy. And if she sounded distraught, there must be something...

In the concierge's office the bellman melted discreetly away. Laura picked up the phone.

"Nancy?" she said.

"Laura," the girl said breathlessly. "Thank goodness. I've been waiting *forever.* Oh, Laura, please come home. I just don't know what to *do.*"

Laura had sudden ominous visions of broken bones, high fevers, masked intruders. "Nancy," she said again. Her own voice was a little shaky. "Calm down. What's the matter?"

"Becky's having a nightmare or a fit or a seizure or something. She woke up screaming and she won't *stop.* Oh, Laura, I can't stay on the phone. She's just *throwing* herself around up there. You have to come right away."

"I will. We both will. But I don't know how long it will take me to find Nick. There must be a million people here. I'll—"

"But it's you she's screaming for. Her mom, anyway. Oh, *God.* It sounds as if she's . . . I have to go."

"Nancy!" Laura said. "Don't—"

Too late. The phone had gone dead.

The bellman materialized in the doorway with suspicious promptness. Obviously he hadn't gone far. "Can I be of any service to you, Mrs. Rafland?" he said.

"Yes," Laura said. "Can I have a pen and paper? I'm going to go back to the ballroom and look for my husband again, but I can't take more than a minute. One of his...one of our little girls is ill. If I leave a note with you, will you look for him, too?"

"Of course, madam," the bellman said soothingly. "The paper is there on the desk. There are pens in the top drawer."

Nick,

I'm going to look for you but I don't have much time so I'm leaving this with the bellman just in case. Nancy called. Becky's had some kind of a nightmare and won't stop screaming. If I don't find you I'm taking a cab home.

Laura

She folded the note once and handed it to the bellman. "Thank you," she said.

Back in the ballroom there seemed to be nothing but a swirling mass of color and movement and music. Almost every man had the same black-and-white evening clothes. At first glance there didn't seem to be any self-assured dark-haired heads standing an inch or two taller than the rest.

And then all of a sudden, against every probability, she saw him.

He wasn't standing but sitting, at a small white wicker table under a fancifully constructed artificial arbor hung with leaves and flowers and twinkling with tiny lights. Laura had actually taken a step toward him when she realized that he wasn't alone.

There was a woman sitting across from him. She was fair-skinned and fair-haired and beautiful. A green taffeta dress and emerald earrings, which probably meant green eyes. As Laura watched, frozen between one step and another, Nick reached across the table and took one of the woman's hands in both of his own.

The woman made no attempt to withdraw her hand. She leaned forward and smiled radiantly and said something. Nick laughed just a little, in that distinctive self-mocking way he had, and—

Laura turned away abruptly.

She was a beautiful creature, I'll give her that. Julie, I mean. Hair as blond as a little girl's. Green eyes...

You're presentable enough as a wife for Nick here, I suppose, even if you can't hold a candle to Julie McAllister...

He even sees them occasionally. Social things. Charity things. Everyone's always very civilized. Very pleasant...

Pleasant, indeed.

Somehow Laura found herself out in the hall again. The bellman was there, just entering the ballroom. He said something to her, a question, but she didn't understand it. She didn't want to understand it. She didn't want to listen to it.

There was a doorman on the Congress Avenue side of the Hyatt, and he called a taxi for her.

Becky was asleep at last, worn out by her irrational nightmare hysterics. Emily, trembling with tension, had been given crackers and cocoa and reassurances and finally coaxed back to sleep as well. Nancy was gone. Laura was exhausted.

Nick had not come home.

Laura closed her bedroom door behind her and leaned against it. For a moment she felt nothing at all. And then, tired as she was, she realized that one small sense impression was filtering through. She could smell the violets.

She opened her eyes. There they were on the dressing table, in their prosaic water glass. Next to them lay the silk moiré box with the moonstone-and-amethyst necklace safely curled away inside. The lavender-purple chiffon dress hung over the back of the chair. In the mirror she could see herself, barefoot, her hair disheveled, wearing the first clothes her hands had fallen on when she had found five minutes to change: faded mulberry-colored riding tights and an oversized gray cotton T-shirt.

She frowned. I don't look much like I looked at the beginning of the evening, she thought. But then nothing's like it was at the beginning of the evening.

I'm being stupid. He was just sitting there talking to her, for heaven's sake. She's been married to another man for fifteen years. *Do you think he would allow himself to go on loving another man's wife?* No, of course not. Not Nick, with his Don Quixote ideals. Of course not.

But she was so beautiful.

. . . even if you can't hold a candle to Julie McAllister.

Behind her there were three sharp raps on the door. Laura jumped as if the blows had struck her directly between her shoulder blades.

"Laura?" It was Nick, of course. "Laura, open the door."

"It's not locked," she said. She took a step away from the door and turned. "Open it yourself."

He did. For once he looked less than impeccable. His jacket was gone. He had pulled his black silk tie loose, and it hung a bit unevenly from either side of his collar. The first three of the onyx studs had been wrenched out of his starched shirt. Under its stiff conventional whiteness his tanned skin and the black hair on his chest looked incongruously vital and male.

"They're all right?" he said. "Becky? Emmie? They both seem to be sleeping perfectly normally."

"They're all right," Laura said. "Becky never would say what she was dreaming about. Too much excitement, I think. And it was the first time we actually left them with a baby-sitter."

"I wonder if they'll ever get over it," Nick said. "This fear of being left behind."

"They will," Laura said. "It'll just take time."

He looked at her for a moment. And then quite deliberately he pulled the door shut behind him. The click of the latch was surprisingly loud in the silence.

"And speaking of being left behind," he said. "Did you really look for me, Laura, back at the Hyatt? Or did you just leave your note with the bellman and go?"

Laura turned her back on him and walked to the window. Her hands felt cold. "I looked for you," she said.

"The bellman told me a very strange story of you just stepping inside the door of the ballroom and then stepping out again so quickly that you almost tripped over him."

"The bellman," Laura said defensively, "seems to have taken his own sweet time about telling you any story at all. It's been over two hours."

"When he saw you leave again so quickly he thought you'd already spoken to me. It was sheer chance that he ran across me later on. I left as soon as he gave me your note, Laura."

"But all that time I was gone and you didn't even know it," Laura said. It sounded childish, but she couldn't help herself. "Didn't you wonder where I was? Didn't you *miss* me?"

He had come up behind her, and she could hear him breathing. He smelled of soap and starch, a little of the outdoors and the night. "Of course I missed you," he said. "But you seemed happy enough on your own. The last time I saw you, you were talking to your newspaper friends. To tell you the truth, after what happened when I...when I gave you the necklace, I thought you were the one who was avoiding me."

She swung around to face him. "I wasn't avoiding you," she said. "I did look for you. I saw you sitting in that arbor thing."

"You *saw* me? For God's sake, Laura, then why didn't you—?"

"You were with her."

"With who?"

All of a sudden her flight from the ballroom seemed as unreasonable as Becky's six-year-old midnight terrors. Laura looked down at her own bare feet on the carpet. "Julie," she said. "Julie McAllister."

He didn't say anything at first, although she heard the steady rhythm of his breathing stop for a moment. Then he put his fingers very gently under her chin and tilted her face up to his. His expression was an odd combination of understanding and wry amusement and something else that Laura couldn't quite identify.

"You don't even know Julie McAllister," he said.

"Nanfran told me what she looked like. It was Julie there in the arbor, wasn't it?"

"Yes," he said. "It was."

"And you were only talking."

"Yes," he said again. "We were only talking."

"You were holding her hand."

"Was I? I don't remember."

"You don't *remember?*"

"What I remember," he said, "is the way you looked in that ravishing violet chiffon dress of yours. Dancing with you, even if it was only once or twice. What I remember is feeling as if I'd been hit in the stomach with a two-by-four when I realized you'd left without me."

"I was worried about Becky."

"I know. It's all right. I'm glad you were here for her."

"And I would have danced with you more than once or twice. I thought you didn't want to dance with me."

He smiled. "We seem to have been at cross purposes tonight," he said.

"I guess we have."

He put his arms around her waist. It was so easy and so natural that Laura didn't have a chance to feel even a flicker of uneasiness. "The evening isn't over yet," he said.

"We can't dance here," she said. "There isn't any music."

"I don't need music. Do you?"

"I don't know. And anyway, I took my dress off an hour ago."

He laughed a little and rested his chin on top of her head. "What a delightful thought," he murmured. "Well, you could always put it back on."

"I don't want to put it back on."

He gathered her a little closer. She could feel the shape of his body inside his clothes, the long muscles of his legs, his hard flat stomach, the depth and breadth of his chest against her own softer, more vulnerable flesh. She could feel him breathing. They swayed very gently in the silence.

"I wasn't really holding hands with Julie McAllister," he said, after a moment. "I think I may have patted her hands at one point. Would you like to know what we were talking about?"

"No."

"I'm going to tell you anyway. We were talking about children. Emmie and Becky and her three. Her oldest boy starts high school in the fall and she's very proud of him. I think that was what generated the hand-patting episode."

"Oh," Laura said.

"You don't really believe me, do you?"

"I believe you. I just wish..."

She hesitated. I wish you had never known her, she thought suddenly. Never loved her, never lost her. I wish you still had all that idealism and passion and romance in your heart, unforfeited, undamaged, untouched, so that you could...

So that you could what?

Nicholson will never, never fall in love with you. Never.

"What do you wish, sweetheart?" he said softly.

She looked up at him. Something was different. Something was missing. Some feeling that went with being touched. It had always been there before but it simply wasn't there anymore. He must have felt the difference, too, because he brought up his hands and cradled her face between his palms and kissed her.

Not a light kiss this time, or a subtle or even a particularly gentle kiss. His mouth caught hers, compelled her lips to part for him. She felt his teeth graze her own teeth, felt his tongue finding and taking for itself all the sweet dark secrets of her mouth. And there were secrets of his own for her to learn, too, the deep complex taste of him, the heat of his mouth, just how far she had to lift her arms to put them around his neck. His hands caressed her throat, her shoulders, slipped up under the looseness of the T-shirt, discovering the smooth bare curves of her back. In a hurry and expecting to be alone, she had pulled the T-shirt on over nothing but naked skin.

"Laura," he said softly. "Laura. Sweetheart. You're going to have to tell me if you want me to stop."

"Yes," she whispered. "No."

His hands skimmed over her back very gently. She felt him smile. "You only get one answer to that question," he said.

"No," she said.

He held her with one arm around her waist, and his other hand moved, the tips of his fingers tracing the curve where her breast lifted away from her body. She shut her eyes. Ah, *now*...

The skin of his palm, warm and smooth and firm, moved over her. The pleasure came as a shock, so intense that she flinched away a little, gasping. He froze. Then his hand moved again, slipped lightly down over the curve of her waist. He laced his fingers together in the small of her back and leaned away.

"Laura," he said again.

She opened her eyes.

Very quietly he said, "Don't you think it's time for you to tell me about it?"

She stared at him mutely. Then without any warning an enormous uncontrollable lump rose in her throat. She ducked her face against the smooth starched whiteness of his shirt and to her horror she started to cry.

"Hush," he said. "Laura. Sweetheart. Don't cry. Don't cry. Just tell me."

"I can't," she said. "Oh, Nick, I've never told anyone. Never. Not even Aunt Grace. It all just sounds like a cheap melodrama anyway."

"A lot of life is that way. Tell me."

She took a breath and lifted her head. "Can we sit down?" she said.

"The bed is the only place where we can both sit here in your charming boudoir," he said with a trace of a smile. "It's about time you and I spent a little time in it together."

"We are not going to spend time in it *together.*"

He pulled her down on the bed beside him and put his arms around her again. "Yes, we are," he said. "Now. Tell me."

It was actually comforting to be close to him, half sitting, half lying on the bed, surrounded by his warmth. She turned her head and pressed her cheek against his sleeve. "I was engaged," she said. "I had just turned eighteen."

"I know. Jefferson Calhoun." His voice was calm, quiet, ordinary. It steadied her.

"Yes," she said. "Jeff. You have to understand, Nick, what it was like. Jeff's mother was a Stephens, you know. A great-great-grandniece of Little Alec Stephens."

"Little Alec who?"

"Stephens. The vice president of the Confederacy. Jeff had old family, you see. He was blond and good-looking.

He was clever. He had beautiful manners, when...when he wanted to use them. He was in the right fraternities and he was good at the right sports and he rode with the hunt."

"A paragon," Nick murmured.

"Aunt Grace didn't like him."

"So she implied in her letters. I'm surprised. He sounds as if he would have been just the kind of boy she would have wanted you to marry."

"At the time she said I was too young. But now that I've seen her...her letters I wonder if she wanted me to get married at all."

"So he was Charleston's golden boy," Nick said. "And your Aunt Grace didn't approve of him. A pretty heady combination for an eighteen-year-old girl."

Laura rubbed her cheek against the fabric of his sleeve. For some reason it felt almost as if she were telling the story of someone else's life. "Being with Jeff made me feel special," she said. "Everyone knew him. Everyone admired him. It made me feel as if I belonged, being Jeff's fiancée. As if I were...loved."

"But you didn't love him."

"No," she said. "I thought I did, of course. He thought I did, too. Poor Jeff. He couldn't comprehend the fact that a girl might not be in love with him. He just thought I was...cold."

"Ah," Nick said softly. "And he made you think so, too."

"It got worse and worse, as the wedding came closer. He wanted to... He thought... Oh, I'm not sure what he thought. Most of the time he was...considerate enough. But that last night..."

She stopped. The sick shrinking feeling was flooding back, as strong as ever. She could feel the tension gathering in Nick's arms and chest as well, feel him straining to reassure her, support her. She shifted her weight uneasily. He loosened his arms a little, but he didn't let her go.

"That last night?" he prompted gently.

For a long moment Laura didn't say anything. Then at ıst she said, "That last night, he...he wasn't considerte."

"Laura. Stop talking like Miss Finesse. Are you trying to ıll me that he raped you?"

She flinched at the word. "No," she said. "No. It didn't o that far. But he...oh, Nick, he *hit* me, and he tore my lothes, and he just kept...just kept...just kept putting his ands on me, and not letting me go, and hurting me, and I as fighting and crying and in such a blind panic that I idn't even know it was Jeff anymore, and finally I was sick. Ie was furious."

"I can imagine," Nick said. There was no emotion in his oice at all. "Then what happened?"

You're not normal, Laura, do you know that? You're not ven human. No flesh-and-blood woman could ever be as old as you've been with me, from the very beginning....

"He left," she said. "He...he said a lot of things to me nd then he left."

"And he was killed...?"

"The next morning. I never saw him again."

"And you never told anyone."

All of a sudden she couldn't bear being in his arms, any ıan's arms, for one more second. Her hands had clenched ıemselves into tight unthinking fists, the same fists she had sed to batter so frantically at Jefferson Calhoun's arms and hest all those years ago. She brought the fists up between er body and Nick's. This time he let her go at once. She tood up so quickly that she almost lost her balance.

"What *good* would it have done?" she said, rounding on im fiercely. "I meant to, at first. I would have had to have aid something, because I couldn't possibly marry him afer that. I was sitting there in my room that next morning rying to find the courage to admit to Aunt Grace that I'd een wrong all along and that we were going to have to canel the wedding at the last minute and recall all the invitaions and...and...and then she came upstairs and she told me that Jeff had been killed. I didn't want to marry him anymore and I was so frightened and so sick and so angry but I didn't want him to be dead. Oh, Nick, I really didn't want him to be *dead.*"

"Of course you didn't," Nick said. "It was an accident."

"A riding accident. And he was wonderful with horses. Born in a saddle, like Emily and Becky. What if he was as upset as I was, and—"

"No," Nick said. "*No,* damn it."

She stared at him.

"Even if he was careless," Nick said more gently, "it wasn't your fault. None of it was your fault. You were young and you were lonely and you thought he was the one, but your body itself, your blood and your bones, knew better. That's all. It was unfortunate but it was no excuse for what he did. You aren't cold now, sweetheart, and you weren't cold then. You just didn't love him."

You weren't cold then. You just didn't love him.

And so if I didn't love him, Laura thought. Her mind was moving with labored unnatural slowness, like a runner in a dream. If I didn't love him and didn't want him to touch me, then what does it mean, Nick, that my blood and my bones did want you to hold me tonight, did want you to kiss me and did want you to touch me? Does that mean that I...?

"Will you come back and sit with me for a little while longer?" Nick said. "Just sit, Laura, that's all."

She hesitated for a moment, and then she sat on the very edge of the bed. He put his arm around her shoulders. There was no sensuality in it. No demand. Just kindness. Affection. Reassurance. A little at a time she relaxed, and at last she let herself lean against him.

"So," he said softly. "You and I are going to have to start from the very beginning."

She swallowed. "I suppose we are," she said. "After what happened with Jeff I could never... There was never anyne else. Never anyone at all. I told you it sounded like a heap melodrama."

"Hush," he said. "You know that's not true."

They sat in silence for a while. Laura kept hearing his ords. *You weren't cold then. You just didn't love him. You eren't cold then. You just didn't love him....*

"Nick?" she said.

"Hmm?"

"I don't know how I feel anymore."

"That's all right, Mrs. Rafland," he said. She could tell om the sound of the words that he was smiling just a lit-e, and that it was one of his characteristic self-mocking niles. "Neither do I."

Chapter Nine

"Aunt Laura?" Emily said. "The mailman wants you to come. He says he needs you to sign a paper or something before he can leave a letter he has."

Laura looked up from the half-written column on her computer screen. Her first thought was of Sharon Scott. Some legal papers for Nick, something to do with the custody suit. She gave Emily a quick hug and followed her to the front door.

"I'm Mrs. Rafland," she said to the mailman. It still sounded odd. "Mr. Rafland isn't here right now, but I'll be happy to—"

"This isn't for him," the mailman said. "It's for you. Sign here, please."

The registered-mail receipt was attached to the back of the white legal-sized envelope. Laura frowned and signed it. The mailman peeled off the card and handed the envelope back to her.

"There you go," he said. "Have a nice day."

On the front of the envelope there was a discreetly en-
raved return address: Fournier and Fournier, Attorneys at
aw. Laura stared at it, frozen. Emily finally thanked the
ailman with solemn aplomb and shut the front door.

"What is it, Aunt Laura?" she said. "Are you all right?
an I get you a drink of water?"

Laura looked up. "No," she said. "No, honey, thank
ou. I'm fine. I just wasn't expecting this. I mean, not so
oon."

"What is it?"

The envelope felt too thick to have just a single sheet of
aper in it. But was it really thick enough to have both a
tter and another envelope, a fifteen-year-old envelope,
nside? Laura tried to slip one finger under the flap, but her
ands had started to shake so badly that she couldn't seem
control them.

"Aunt Laura?" Emily's voice had turned anxious. "Are
ou sure you're all right? Would you like me to open that for
ou?"

Somehow Laura managed to thrust the envelope down
nto the pocket of her loose linen blazer. "Go get Becky,"
he said. "Quick. We're going to drive downtown."

Emily's face lit up. "To Uncle Nick's office?" she said.

"Yes," Laura said. "To your Uncle Nick's office."

The Rafland Group occupied the whole top floor of a
uilding at the intersection of Sixth Street and Congress
venue. Emily and Becky waved blithely to the receptionist
nd ran down the hall toward Nick's private office in the
orthwest corner. Laura followed more slowly. The drive
ad steadied her briefly, but now her hands were shaking
gain. Her head ached. She felt dizzy and a little sick. The
tter in her pocket seemed to make a faint crinkling sound
ith every step she took.

Nick's office door was closed. Laura could hear the girls
aughing and chattering in the office next to it. She paused
nd looked in.

"Laura. Hi. When these two showed up I figured you couldn't be more than a few steps behind." It was Christina Jaramillo, Nick's secretary. "I'm sorry, but he's—"

"—just finished with his meeting," Nick said from the hall at Laura's back. Hearing his soft deep voice was such an enormous relief that Laura's knees actually felt weak for a moment, and a ring of unnatural brightness trembled at the edge of her vision. When she tried to turn she wavered, and all of a sudden his hand was under her elbow, steady as stone.

"Are you all right?" she heard him say. "Come in and sit down. Tina, would you get some water, please?"

There seemed to be no lapse of time at all, but when Laura opened her eyes she was sitting in a deep square chair with a glass of water on the table beside her. There was ice in the glass. Her mouth felt cold. Apparently she had been drinking the water. In the office next door she could hear voices, Nick's and Christina's, Emily's and Becky's, just murmurs, unintelligible. Her vision cleared. Then Nick walked into the office and shut the door behind him. Concern was evident in his dark eyes.

"So," he said quietly. "Tell me about your mysterious letter."

She took the letter out of her pocket and handed it to him mutely.

"Fournier and Fournier," he said. "That's what I thought." He handed it back to her. "Well, go ahead. Open it."

"Oh, Nick, I don't know if I can."

"It's only a piece of paper. I'm surprised that you'd let it frighten you into a faint."

Laura sat up straighter. "I'm not frightened," she said. "And I didn't faint."

He smiled at her. "Amazon," he said. "That's more like it."

She took a deep breath and looked at the envelope one last time. Then she tore open a corner of the flap, slipped her finger into the opening, and ripped the envelope across. Ripped it, in fact, completely in half.

Nick grinned. "You give me hope," he said. "It obviously takes you a while to make up your mind to do something, but when you finally do it you do it with real passion."

Laura flushed. "It's a letter," she said a little stiffly. "From Edward Fournier. 'Dear Mrs. Rafland. Allow me to offer you my best wishes. . . .' Et cetera, et cetera. And—"

She held up a smaller envelope made of pale gray linen-textured paper. The flap was sealed.

"Aha," Nick said. "Another opportunity for me to observe your provocative envelope-opening technique."

"Oh, hush," Laura said. "I don't want to tear this one. Do you have a letter opener?"

He got up and walked over to his desk and picked up a silver stiletto. "This gets better and better," he said. "Here."

Laura put the point of the knife under the flap. What am I wishing for? she thought. My father's name? Some kind of reassurance that the 'unfortunate weakness' Aunt Grace was so concerned about is really just a nineteenth-century figment of her imagination? Or am I wishing against all the odds for the words I never heard her say when she was alive?

I love you, Laura Lavinia.

I love you, I love you, my own flesh and blood, my daughter, my child. . . .

The knife was sharper than she expected it to be, and sliced precipitously through the gray envelope. There was a single sheet of matching gray writing paper inside. Laura's hands had started to shake again. Very carefully she unfolded the letter.

Dear Laura,

This is not an easy letter for me to write, but as you know I have already had two small strokes and I cannot take the chance that you might marry and have children of your own without knowing certain facts.

You are my own natural child. I arranged the adoption as a means to avoid censure and distress for both of us. There was no question of a marriage between your father and me.

Your father's name is Daniel Eldon. His mother was said to have died of pneumonia, but the truth was that in secret she drank alcohol to excess. Her grandfather, an uncle and one of her brothers were also widely known to be uncontrollably heavy drinkers, and violent with it.

I have done my best to bring you up in a temperate and methodical manner, so that you might avoid this taint. I have tried to convince you that it might be best if you did not marry at all, but if you are reading this letter you have not heeded my warnings. I can only implore you to watch carefully for any suggestion of the Eldons' bad blood in your own children.

Please forgive me, my dear, for everything. You were a light in darkness for me.

Grace Gardiner

"A taint," Laura whispered, unbelieving. "Bad blood. I was right."

Nick frowned. "What kind of a taint?" he said.

She handed him the letter. He scanned it quickly and then read it over again, slowly and carefully. "Drinking alcohol to excess," he said at last. "Going back three generations. God in heaven, did she really think it could be... I know they're doing research on genetic predispositions, Laura, but it's hardly some kind of bad blood that you automatically inherit. And it's certainly not something to keep you from marrying and having children of your own. Forgive me, but that's the worst kind of old-fashioned prejudice."

"I know," Laura said. "I told you she had some nineteenth-century attitudes. Poor Aunt Grace. Poor Daniel

Eldon. I wonder if he...'drank alcohol to excess.' I wonder if that's why he was hedonistic and disorderly. If that's why she wouldn't marry him."

"I wonder," Nick said, "if he was ever really hedonistic and disorderly at all. Or if it was just that he wasn't what she calls 'temperate and methodical.' I wonder if he's still alive. Your...your Aunt Grace was what? In her seventies when she died?"

"Seventy-six," Laura said. "If they were about the same age he could still be alive. It's all right for you to say 'my mother,' Nick."

He smiled at her. Her heart contracted. "Listen," he said. "Now that we know his name, it would be easy enough for me to—"

"Excuse me. Nick?"

It was Christina Jaramillo. Nick looked up.

"Mike Lyle is on the phone," Christina said. "He says it's very important. And Mr. Goodmark is going to be here in ten minutes."

Laura got up. "I'm interrupting you," she said. "And the girls must be driving you crazy, Tina. Give me the letter, Nick. I'm all right now. I really am."

He handed her the letter. She folded it and put it back in its envelope and pressed it between her fingers. *Your father's name is Daniel Eldon.... You were a light in darkness for me.*

There's nothing wrong with me, Laura thought. Not really. And I have a father. And my mother loved me. Now if only Nick could...

If only Nick could what?

"Don't leave yet," he said. "Go ahead and put Mike through, Tina."

Laura sat down again. Mike Lyle, she thought. I've heard Nick talk about him before. He's... Oh. Yes. The attorney. The one who talked to Sharon Scott. He was supposed to be filing the custody suit in California.

The telephone on the desk made a discreet electronic purring sound. Nick reached over and touched a button.

"Mike," he said. "I've got you on speaker because Laura's here. What's up?"

"You're not going to like it," Mike Lyle said. He had a quick light voice with no trace of a Texas accent. "I had one of my people try to serve some papers on Sharon Scott today, and she's disappeared."

"Disappeared?" Nick said.

"Disappeared?" Laura said, at the same time.

"Without a trace."

Nick stood up and walked to the windows. "Do you think something's happened to her?" he said.

"Nope. She quit her job. Turned off her phone and utilities. All nice and neat. She left under her own power, Nick. Just no forwarding address. You know what I think?"

"You think she's coming here," Laura said suddenly. "You think she may try to... try to see the girls."

"I don't know," Mike Lyle said. "But there's something damned strange about it. First she doesn't want any part of them for six years, then all of a sudden she's worried about who's bringing them up. Then she asks for money. Then she cuts and runs. It doesn't add up. But I'd keep a real close eye on those kids, if I were you. At least until we find out for sure where she is and what she's up to."

"You're looking for her?" Nick said. He had turned and was walking back across the office. There was a little spark of ferocity in his dark eyes that Laura had never seen before. "Whatever it takes. No limits."

"I know," Mike Lyle said. "I'll keep you posted."

Nick touched the button on the telephone again and the line went dead. "Take them home," he said. "Not to the house, to the ranch. I'll call Nanfran. I want one or the other of you to be with them every minute."

Laura hesitated. She could hear the girls laughing with Tina in the outer office. "Are you coming?" she said.

"I can't. Not right away. I'll get there as soon as I can. I trust you, Laura."

That was all. *I trust you, Laura.*

It was at that precise moment that it all came clear. *I trust you* was good, as far as it went. *I will care for you in my own way* was good, too, and so was *What I remember is the way you looked in that ravishing violet chiffon dress.* But none of it was enough.

He had already half turned away and was touching the buttons on the phone again. Laura stared at him, at his dark bony profile, the distinctive oblique setting of his eyes, the clear-cut sensual shape of his mouth and the way his heavy black hair was neatly barbered at the back of his neck. She stared at him as if she were seeing him for the first time, and she realized that what she really wanted to hear more than anything else in the world was something he was never going to say.

What she really wanted to hear was *I love you.*

It was the letter, Laura thought. The letter from my mother was what cleared the last of the shadows away.

You were a light in darkness to me.

The little lake was summer-warm at last. Every trace of the shivaree, the tire marks of the pickup truck and the footprints of the Thundering Herd, her own tracks and Nick's, had long since vanished from its sandy verge. Penny picked her way through the shallow water with the delicacy of a dancer. Laura sat back in the saddle and let her feet dangle free of the stirrups and looked up at the narrow crescent of the moon.

And so Grace Gardiner was my mother, she thought, my blood, all along. I was never really alone. And she did love me. Because of who she was and what she believed she was never able to be anything but kind of a make-believe . . . A make-believe mother. Oh, God, she would have expired on the spot if anyone had ever called her "Mom." But she did love me. She did love me. I know that now.

A light in darkness.

And now I know who my father was, too. Daniel Eldon. Daniel Eldon.

"Daniel Eldon," Laura said aloud. The syllables felt ill-assorted and awkward, as if they weren't really a name at all. "Daniel Eldon. Are you still alive? Did you love her? Why wouldn't she marry you? Why wouldn't she tell you about me?"

There was no answer, of course. Penny swiveled her ears and snorted softly.

"I can't face it yet, Penny," Laura said. "It's all too...too enormous. But maybe in a few months, when I've had a chance to get used to it, I'll go to Charleston and see if he's still there. Maybe Nick and the girls and I can..."

She stopped. She had promised herself not to think about Nick but there he was, dark and steady and purposeful as ever. How strange love is, she thought. For so long I believed I had no love at all, and now all of a sudden I have more than I can quite cope with. My mother's love. This unnerving new love of my own, a love that I never dreamed I'd be able to feel. How am I ever going to be able to keep him from knowing? Because love was definitely not part of our arrangement....

Penny lifted her head and whickered. Laura blinked and came back to herself, and there at the edge of the lake she saw him.

He was too far away for her to see his expression clearly. Keno, saddleless and wearing only a hackamore, was grazing idly about fifty feet away. Involuntarily Laura leaned forward, toward the still dark figure. Penny responded immediately, splashing through the water halfway between a trot and a canter. When she reached the sand Nick put out his hand and caught one of her reins, just below the snaffle ring.

"I've been calling the house," he said. His eyes were dark and glittering with tension, although his voice was deep and soft and level as always. "All afternoon and all evening."

"The girls are safe," Laura said. "They're with Nanfran. Janet's there, too, with Kelsey and Derek and Jared."

"I know," he said. "I was looking for you."

Laura struggled to keep her voice under control. "I just needed some time to myself," she said. "Some time to think about... about the letter. About everything."

He looked away for a moment. The long tendons in his throat stood out in sharp relief. Then he turned his head and looked at her again. "Laura," he said. "Get down. Please."

She sat there, frozen. Penny stood, still as a rock.

"Laura," he repeated very softly. *"Get down."*

It was impossible to look away from him. In a movement that seemed to go on forever Laura swung her right leg over the front of the saddle. One moment of hesitation. And then she kicked the stirrup away and let herself slide down into his arms.

He caught her around the waist before her feet could touch the sand. Her mouth was just above his, and she could feel his body against hers, tense, hard. She shivered suddenly and closed her eyes. He kissed her very lightly. Then he lowered her the rest of the way and the ground was reassuringly solid under her feet and his arms were reassuringly tight around her body.

"Laura," he said, his voice muffled against her hair. "God in heaven. I was worried about you."

"I'm perfectly safe," Laura said. The shivering hadn't gone away. It had just withdrawn to the innermost depths of her body. *It's the shivering,* Becky had said so artlessly, *that does it....* "Sharon Scott isn't going to try to kidnap me."

"Don't say that. Don't even think it. Nobody's going to kidnap anybody. You were just so upset this morning. I hated having to let you bring the girls out here all by yourself."

"It's all right," she said. "I told you. I just wanted to be alone for a little while."

He let her go. "Do you still want to be alone?" he said.

She could feel her response continuing to unfold, step by step. All over her body her skin felt new and thin and very fragile. With each breath the fabric of her clothes, silk and lace, cotton and denim, made faint provocative scrapes of texture against her flesh.

"No," she said. It took an effort to breathe and speak normally. "I was about to come home anyway. What time is it?"

"I don't know." He took her left hand in his and traced the circle of the moonstone ring with one finger. "Laura. Let's not go back quite yet."

"Nick. I don't know if I—"

"Pretend, then," he said, with sudden abrupt intensity. "*Damn* it, Laura, just this once, just for a few minutes, will you at least *pretend* that you want to touch me?"

For a moment neither one of them moved. He was still holding her hand, and despite the harsh sound of his voice it would have been easy enough to slip her fingers out of his. Easy enough to walk away. The sounds of the night, the water, the browsing horses, were suddenly very loud.

"You can't really mean that," Laura said.

"Try me," he said softly. "Oh, just try me, sweetheart."

Silence again. Then Laura lifted her chin. I promised, she thought. He's never going to love me but I've known that from the beginning. He is my husband. He's been so kind and so patient all these weeks. Touching him isn't really that daunting anymore. In fact, touching him is...

"I don't have to pretend, Nick," she said steadily. "Not anymore. Stand still."

She drew her hand out of his and reached up and very deliberately unbuttoned the first button on his shirt. He made a slight movement, just the beginning of a gesture, surprise, negation. She stopped and waited. After a second or two he was still again.

She unbuttoned another button, and another. She finished unbuttoning the shirt and pulled it free of his jeans. Under the weathered blue cotton were the taut heavy muscles of his chest and stomach. She laid one palm lightly against his chest, fascinated by the pale star shape of her hand against his tanned skin and the way the black hair parted around her fingers.

"Laura—" he said.

"Shh," she said. "Stand still."

She put her arms around his waist, under the loose tails of the shirt. Her forehead fit neatly between his collarbones, against the smooth patch of skin at the base of his throat. She could feel his pulse, strong and quick. She turned her head so that her cheek was pressed against his heart.

"Now you pretend," she whispered. "You pretend that you want to touch me."

She wasn't sure what he would do. For a moment he didn't do anything. Then he lifted his hand, and she felt him pull out one of the little tortoiseshell combs she used to hold back her hair.

"Your hair was coming loose," he said. His voice sounded as if he had been running. "Do you have another one of these on the other side? Let me see."

She took a breath and turned her head, and he pulled out the other comb. "There," he said. "Now you match. God, Laura, you have such beautiful hair. I've lain awake at night, you know, thinking about your hair."

He dropped the combs and ran his fingers up into her hair on either side of her face, tilting her head back. "Your hair," he murmured. He bent his head and kissed her, gently at first, and then with a swift profound intensity that dissolved all her strength into hot liquid weakness. "And your mouth."

Laura felt her hands loosen, her arms fall away from his waist. His lips moved very softly over her throat, and then pressed against the curve of her breast. Through the fabric of her T-shirt she felt his breath, hot against her skin. "And your skin," he said softly. "Oh, all of your skin."

"N-Nick?"

"Hmm?"

"You're cheating."

"Cheating how?"

"You're not pretending."

He laughed softly. "To my indescribable shock and amazement," he said, "neither are you. Stand still."

Very slowly he kissed her again, coaxing her mouth open, tasting her one leisurely fraction at a time. No longer was he something entirely new for her to learn. There was a reassuring familiarity about his touch and taste and scent, while at the same time his mouth hinted at newer and even more tantalizing pleasures to be discovered. She reached up and caught hold of his wrists.

"Nick?" Her voice was steadier this time.

"Hmm?"

"Maybe we should pretend to go back to the house."

"Just what I was thinking, Mrs. Rafland."

She opened her eyes and looked at him. His skin seemed to be drawn more tightly over the bones of his face, emphasizing their shape. He smiled at her and pressed her palm against his cheek, and under his skin she felt a very faint pulse, nerve-deep, a tremor of awareness and expectation.

"Penny and Keno are probably halfway down the road by now," he said. "Come on. Let's go find them."

If this were a book, Laura thought wryly, we would have come straight home together and kept on pretending... oh, anything we wanted to pretend. Everything we wanted to pretend. Instead we had to do all the ordinary practical things first.

We had to stop at Nanfran's and pick up Emily and Becky. Nick had to see that the horses were fed and groomed and bedded down. I had to get the girls undressed and into bed and supplied with glasses of water and back into bed. I had to be a mom. A real mom. But now I think they're down for good. And Nick should be finished with the horses soon....

The house was silent. Laura walked down the stairs. A file folder had been tossed on the table just inside the front door. Tossed in careless haste, apparently, because the contents were spilling out haphazardly. Sheets of lined yellow paper. A white envelope with a red-and-blue triangle design that looked like an airplane ticket. A second identical envelope had fallen to the floor. Idly she picked it up.

Her own name jumped out at her.

But I'm not going anywhere, she thought. This must be a mistake. A business trip of Nick's, and Tina's mixed up the names.

She opened the envelope.

It was a first-class ticket, round-trip, from Austin to Charleston. There was a connection in Atlanta. The departure date was August 7 and the return date was August 13.

She put the envelope down on the table and picked up the other one. It was another ticket, just the same, this time for Nick himself.

"But I don't want to go to Charleston," she said aloud. "Not next week. Not so soon."

She broke off. Another name had jumped out at her. This time it was written on one of the loose sheets of paper, in Nick's clear even handwriting.

Daniel Eldon.

She closed her eyes for a moment. Then she opened them again. The name was still there.

There were other words as well. An address in Charleston. A telephone number with an 803 area code. Fragments of sentences, quite obviously notes from a telephone conversation.

Daniel Eldon. Impressionist painter. Day job carpenter, Christmas 1962. No idea of pregnancy. Married 1966. Son and two daughters. One granddaughter...

Laura was still staring at the sheet of paper when she heard Nick open the back door. His boot heels clicked against the polished white oak of the hallway. Then they stopped. For a long time there was silence. She couldn't bring herself to look up.

"Laura?" he said at last.

The words on the paper were blurring in the most peculiar way. Laura blinked. A drop of something wet fell on the paper. In a small irregular circle the black ink feathered away to gray.

"Oh, God," he said. "Don't cry. I was so upset when I came in this evening that I just threw everything down without thinking that... Laura, I'm sorry. I meant to tell you about it, not just leave it there for you to find. Will you let me explain?"

"You called him," Laura whispered. "You yourself, without telling me. Without me there. You *talked* to him. My...my father. You *told* him about me. You even decided that we should go there."

"I'm sorry," he said again. "I never meant for it to go so far. There was a break in my meeting and I called information in Charleston, just to see what I could find out. There he was. I never dreamed it would be so easy. And the information operators connect you now. All of a sudden the phone had rung and Daniel Eldon himself had answered it and—"

"You could have just hung up," she said.

"I could have," he said slowly. "I see now that I should have. Laura. Look at me."

She put the paper down on the table and scrubbed her fingers across her cheeks. Then she shook back her hair and looked up at him. He had half buttoned his shirt and tucked the tails neatly back into his jeans but otherwise he was the same Nick she had walked away from the lake with less than an hour before, meaning to...meaning to...

Impossible now, of course. Impossible.

"You were so upset this morning," he said. His face was white under his tan. "You came to me. You seemed to want...help, support, I don't know, something, when you opened the letter. Somehow I thought I could give you the same support if I—"

"But you didn't have any *right,*" Laura said, cutting him off for a second time. It was rude, of course, and her voice was getting louder and her thoughts were getting less coherent, but she couldn't seem to make herself stop. Too much had come clear that had never been clear before, about Grace Gardiner, about Daniel Eldon, about Nick himself and her own heart.

"You didn't have any right to interfere," she went on hotly. "To put yourself between me and my...my father. To find out things about him before you were even sure I wanted to know. You may be my husband and I may have come to you this morning and you can talk all you want to about helping and supporting and caring and... and pretending, but the truth is that you don't love me and you've never loved me and—"

"Oh, no. *No.*"

It was a tiny tear-choked voice from just above them, and insubstantial as it was it cut through Laura's rush of words like a knife. Laura and Nick turned in a single movement. Emily was crouched behind the railing at the center landing of the switchback staircase. She had an empty drinking glass in her hand.

"Don't say that, Aunt Laura," she quavered. "Please don't say that. About not loving, I mean."

"Emily," Laura said. "Oh, Emily." Without quite being aware of what she was doing she found herself crouching on the landing with the little girl's trembling body clasped fiercely in her arms. Nick was there, too, and he had his arms around them both.

"I didn't mean it," Laura said. "Truly I didn't. I was just having a tantrum like Becky does, and saying things I shouldn't have. Don't cry. Don't cry. Oh, Emily, honey, don't cry."

"I spilled the water," Emily sobbed. "I wanted another drink and I spilled the water and I thought I should come and tell you and you were *fighting* and maybe Derek was *right.*"

"Maybe Derek was right about what, honey?" Laura said.

"Nothing. Nothing. *Nothing.*"

"We weren't fighting," Nick said gently. "Not really. I just did something very thoughtless and very unfair to your Aunt Laura, and she was upset. She had every right to be upset. But I told her I was sorry and it's over and done with and we're not going to fight anymore. Are we, Laura?"

He was saying all the right things. *I was thoughtless. I was unfair. She had every right to be upset. I'm sorry.*

All the right things but one.

I do love her and I've always loved her....

Laura bent her head. Her combs had been lost forever in the sand by the little lake and her hair fell forward, hiding her face. "No," she said hopelessly. "We're not going to fight anymore."

Chapter Ten

"Mom?" Becky said. She put down her breakfast toast and leaned forward on her elbows. Her dark eyes were troubled. "Derek says you and Uncle Nick can't really be married."

"Shut *up,*" Emily said, with a rare flash of temper. "I told you not to tell them about that."

"Shh, Emily," Laura said quietly. She turned back to Becky. "Why on earth does Derek think your Uncle Nick and I can't be married, honey?"

"'Cause you have two different rooms. We were all talking about our rooms last night and Derek has to share a room with Jared and he doesn't like it. I told him that Emily and I have our own rooms all to ourselves and that even you and Uncle Nick have your own rooms. And he said you couldn't really be married, then."

Laura looked down at her coffee cup for a moment. "Rooms," she said, in a carefully neutral voice, "don't have anything to do with it. Of course we're really married. Your Uncle Nick told you that, the very first morning."

"See?" Emily said crossly. There were faint violet smudges of sleeplessness under her eyes. "I told you so."

Becky still looked doubtful. "But Derek says—" she began.

"You pay no attention to what Derek says." It was Nick's voice, from the kitchen. "At the ripe old age of nine he's hardly an expert on marriage. Good morning, sweetheart."

He bent and kissed the top of Laura's head as he passed behind her. The kiss and the endearment were probably deliberately calculated to reassure the girls, to satisfy Emily in particular after last night's disaster. It had taken over an hour to get her back to sleep. And then, Laura thought, then Nick and I simply went off to our own-rooms-all-to-ourselves as if those moments by the lake had never happened at all.

She ran her fingers nervously through her hair. There almost seemed to be a concentration of heat at the spot where his lips had touched so briefly. "Good morning," she said.

"Uncle Nick, are we going to go back to our other house after breakfast?" Becky demanded. "We're supposed to go to the Nature Center this afternoon, you know."

"Not today," Nick said mildly. He looked tired but there was no trace of strain in his soft deep voice. "I want you all to stay here at the ranch for a while."

Becky's brows drew together in her familiar scowl. "Well, I want to go to the Nature Center," she said. "We're only s'posed to be here at the ranch on weekends."

"I know," Nick said. "I'm sorry. Your Aunt Laura and I will take you to the Nature Center next week. But today you have to—"

"No," Becky said. "I don't want to. I won't."

"Everything's all *wrong,*" Emily burst out with sudden passionate anguish. "We can't go back to our other house and you and Aunt Laura were fighting last night and Derek says you're not really married and nothing's ever going to be right ever *again.*"

She pushed back her chair and ran out of the room. Becky stared after her for a moment, her own fit of pique forgotten. Then she turned to Nick. "Y-you and Mom weren't fighting last night," she said in a small apprehensive voice. "Were you?"

"No," Nick said.

"No," Laura said, at the same time.

Nick even smiled at little at that. "You see?" he said. "Your...Mom and I are in perfect agreement with each other. We may have had a small disagreement last night, sweetheart, but we weren't fighting. Not the way you mean it. Grown-ups just have different ideas about things sometimes."

"Oh," Becky said. She didn't look convinced. "May I be excused, please?"

Before either one of them could answer she was gone. Laura started to get up, but Nick reached across the table and put his hand on her arm. "Don't," he said gently. "Just saying the same thing to them over and over isn't going to do any good right now. Let them have a little time to themselves."

"Emily's right, you know," Laura said. "Everything has turned out wrong. Everything."

"That's a pretty sweeping statement."

"We should have known that it wouldn't work. I should have known. I was insane to agree to it."

"Laura," he said. "Stop it. That's exactly what Emmie and Becky are feeling, you know. What they're reacting to. Your own confusion. Your own doubt."

"I'm not confused," Laura said defensively. "I can see the whole situation perfectly clearly. I'm a make-believe mom and a make-believe wife and ... and a make-believe daughter, too. I wasn't even the one to have the first conversation with my own father."

"I'm sorry," Nick said. "I'm sorry I called him. I'm sorry I talked to him. I'm sorry I bought the tickets. I thought I was doing something to help you. I thought I was doing something to please you. God in heaven, Laura, if saying it a thousand times will help, I'll say it a thousand times. If saying—"

He stopped. Some thought of his own had surprised him.

"But that's not what you want to hear, is it?" he went on slowly. "Me saying I'm sorry."

"No," she whispered. "That's not what I want to hear."

Silence.

"The words would be easy," he said at last.

She took a shaky breath and put her napkin down. "I don't want the words," she said. "The words with no meaning behind them."

He hesitated again. The whole world hesitated.

Laura stood up. She felt weightless. Laura-on-the-inside seemed to have gone away somewhere, leaving nothing but a thin fragile Miss Finesse shell behind.

"Never mind," she said. Even her voice sounded dry and light. "I was upset yesterday and I'm tired this morning but that's all. I didn't mean it. I didn't mean any of it."

Nick stood up, too. "Laura," he said. "Don't. Please don't."

"Are you going to go to the office today? I'm a few columns ahead so I can stay here with the girls."

"I have to go in. I have meetings again. And Eleanor Kinnard's coming over this afternoon with a battalion of lawyers and the final papers on the land deal. Laura—"

"Did you hear everything Becky said? All of Derek's worldly wisdom on marriage and bedrooms?"

"Yes," he said. "I heard it."

"I'm going to move my things into your room today. I hope you don't mind."

"Of course I don't mind," he said. "But for God's sake, Laura, do you think that's what I want? To be an *obligation* to you?"

"I'll see you this evening," she said. "Good luck with Eleanor Kinnard."

She turned away, so empty, so weightless that her feet barely seemed to touch the floor, and walked out of the room.

The eerie lightness went away little by little as the morning progressed. After all, it was hard to feel light and detached when you were carrying armfuls of clothes from one closet to another, dividing up drawer space and rearranging towels and toothbrushes in the bathroom. Laura hadn't so much as set foot in the master suite since the night of the shivaree. My wedding night, she said to herself deliberately, wondering if the memory would call up any response, any emotion.

It didn't.

By noon a summer storm seemed to be brewing and the air was close and heavy. As they ate their lunch Emily and Becky were still subdued. Eventually they wandered out to the yard at the side of the house and began a desultory game with their Barbie dolls under the bois d'arc trees. Laura took her computer to the screened-in corner of the veranda where she could watch them and call them in if it started to rain.

There was no warning, no sound of a car's engine or plume of red dust from the driveway. Laura simply looked up between one typed line and the next and the strange woman was there. Emily and Becky were staring up at her. Even from the veranda Laura could tell that they were puzzled and a bit apprehensive. Emily said something and pointed at the house. The woman shook her head. Then she crouched down and reached for Emily's hand.

Laura was on her feet and through the door and down the steps before she realized what she was doing. She was halfway across the yard by the time the door slammed behind her. The woman looked up. Laura had a fleeting impression of blue eyes and brilliant coral-colored lipstick and hair too whitely blond to be real.

"Aunt L-Laura," Emily faltered. "This lady says..."

"Who are you?" Laura demanded. She had Emily safely by one hand and Becky by the other. Both girls pressed against her, and it was a little hard to tell if they were trembling or if her own legs were shaking with tension and shock. "What are you doing? How did you get here?"

"I was just telling Emily," the woman said. She had a self-consciously husky voice, and she sounded nervous. "I'm...well, I'm her mother. Her mother and Becky's. My name is Sharon Scott."

"You are not," Becky said. "Miss Finesse is our mother. Not anybody named Sharon anything."

"But I am Miss Finesse," Sharon Scott said. "At least, I—"

"Are *not,*" Becky contradicted her fiercely. "Mom's Miss Finesse. Mom's our mother, too. So there."

"But she isn't really," Emily said in a very small voice.

"She is," Becky said. "She *is.*"

"She's not," Emily said. "She and Uncle Nick don't even—"

"Emily," Laura said steadily. "Becky. Run in the house. Call Nanfran. You know her number. Tell her that I'd like her to come over right away. Tell her that a lady named Sharon Scott is here."

"Don't w-want to go in the house," Becky said. She had started to cry. "Want to stay here with y-you."

"Emily," Laura said desperately. "Take your sister. Go in the house."

Emily looked up at her. There was anguished uncertainty in her eyes. "Are you coming?" she said.

"In a minute, honey."

"Is . . . is she coming?"

"No," Laura said. "Go, Emily. Hurry."

"It's all right," Sharon Scott said. "You don't have to send them away. I only want to—"

"I don't care what you want," Laura said vehemently. "Emily. Becky. It's about to rain anyway. *Go in the house.*"

With one last frightened look, Emily took Becky's hand and the two of them ran toward the veranda door.

"Now," Laura said, swinging around to face Sharon Scott again. "If you have something to say, say it and go. I'm Laura Rafland. Mrs. Nicholson Rafland. And the Black Moon is private property. My mother-in-law will be here in a minute, and if you don't leave I swear we'll call the police."

"She said you were Miss Finesse."

"I am. I took over the column after you were gone."

"Two Miss Finesses. Two Raflands. Twins, even. Kind of weird. Like fate or something."

"You didn't come here to talk about fate. What do you want?"

Sharon Scott looked at her measuringly. After a moment she said, "Kit always said Nick would never get married."

"And I'm sure you were counting on that," Laura said, "when you concocted your little scheme to blackmail him."

"I never meant to blackmail anybody," Sharon said. She sounded surprised, and a trace of East Texas started to break through the practiced huskiness of her voice. "I never meant Emily and Becky any harm. I never meant anybody any harm."

"How can you *say* that?" Laura demanded furiously. "You abandoned them and ignored them for six years, and when Kit was killed and Nick tried to adopt them you refused to sign the papers even though you must have known that was what Kit wanted. You threatened to take them away from Nick. You used them to try to extort money from him. And then you dropped out of sight and came sneaking in here.... Where's your car? You must have a car."

"It's down the road a mile or so," Sharon said. "I walked the rest of the way. I didn't want anyone to know I was here."

"And if I hadn't been watching them—"

"I didn't come here to take them away, if that's what you think," Sharon said. The Texas accent was getting stronger.

"I didn't mean to see anybody or talk to anybody out here. But there they were under the tree with their dollies and I was... I was just curious, that's all."

The screen door hadn't slammed again. Laura glanced over her shoulder. The girls had disappeared. For once they must have let themselves into the house without slamming the door. Oh, Nanfran, Laura thought, *hurry*.

"If you didn't mean to see anybody or talk to anybody," she said to Sharon Scott, "why did you come here at all?"

"I wanted to leave this," Sharon said. She opened the flap of her shoulder bag and took out a plain white business envelope, worn and creased and a little grubby, thick with folded papers.

For a fraction of a second Laura was back at the Driskill, that very first Friday afternoon. She was holding a silver spoon in her hand and Nick was standing in front of her speaker's podium, dark and formidable and so singularly out of place in the middle of an Austin League ladies' luncheon. He had given her an envelope just like the one Sharon Scott was holding. Just like it, but fresh and crisp and new...

"Take it," Sharon was saying. "I meant to sign them all along, you know. It was Howard who didn't want me to."

Laura snatched the envelope and tore it open. *Another opportunity for me to observe your provocative envelope-opening technique....* The adoption agreement was inside. It had been signed and witnessed and notarized in a perfectly legitimate and straightforward fashion.

"Hey, are you all right?" Sharon said. "You look like you're about to pass out."

"I don't understand," Laura said faintly. "Oh, God, we've been so worried.... Who's Howard?"

"My boyfriend," Sharon said. "My ex-boyfriend now, I guess." She lifted her hand halfway to her cheek, stopped herself, and let it drop again. "I moved to California to be with him. He's a lawyer, you see, so when I first heard Kit was dead I asked him what it meant. About the girls, I mean. I was going to call Nick right away. But Howard said not to. He said he'd look into it for me and tell me what to do."

"And do you always do what Howard tells you to do?"

Again Sharon made that odd half gesture with her hand. Suddenly Laura found herself wondering about the unfashionable heaviness of the makeup on Sharon's smooth face and throat.

"Not anymore," Sharon said. "But I did then. It was Howard's idea to ask for the money. He said Nick could afford it. But then Nick wouldn't pay and Howard started saying crazy things and I realized that I had to get away from him. I didn't mean to cause more trouble by not telling anybody where I was going. I just didn't want Howard to be able to find me before I could give you those papers."

Laura stared at her. *There's something damned strange about this whole deal,* Mike Lyle had said so irritably. But now it made sense. Just add one greedy unscrupulous boyfriend in the background and all of a sudden it all made sense.

Sharon Scott lifted her chin slightly. "I know you think I'm the lowest form of life," she said. "But I gave them away six years ago and I don't want to interfere with them now. Nick's as close to their own father as any man could be. He wants them. He loves them. I'm just . . . just sorry I made it harder for everybody by not standing up to Howard Stringer from the very beginning."

"Sharon," Laura said gently. The papers were securely in her hands, real, physical, signed and safe. The girls were safe. "Would you like to come in the house? Have a cup of coffee? Nick isn't here, but I'd like to call him and—"

"No," Sharon said. "I walked up here like I did because I didn't want to see Nick Rafland. I didn't want to have to explain myself. I am what I am and I did what I did and all the talk in the world isn't going to change it. I've done my best to make it right. Now I just want to go."

"Where are you going? Back to California?"

"I'm going someplace where you can't find me and Nick with all his lawyers and investigators can't find me and Howard Stringer for sure can't find me. Now that you've got your precious papers what difference does it make?"

"It makes a difference," Laura said. "It will make a difference to Nick, too, when he hears the whole story. And anyway, look at the weather. It's going to—"

"I don't give a damn about the weather," Sharon Scott said fiercely. "And I don't want you and Nick Rafland feeling sorry for me, either. I never wanted any children in the first place and I don't want them now. So just leave me alone. Leave me *alone.*"

She turned away suddenly. Laura took a step or two after her and stopped. No, she thought. No, Sharon, I won't argue with you now. But someday, someday when the girls are older and more secure... Oh, Sharon, you don't know Nick Rafland very well if you truly think you can find a place where his lawyers and his investigators won't be able to find you.

Nick. I've got to call Nick.

I've got to call Nanfran. She should have been here by now.

I've got to find the girls. Maybe we can go back to town tonight and they can go to the Nature Center tomorrow....

Sharon was already halfway down the driveway. Laura ran across the yard and took the veranda steps two at a time. The screen door slammed behind her. She opened the double glass doors to the dining room. "Emily!" she called. "Becky! Where are you?"

There was no answer. They weren't in the kitchen or the family room or the living room. Upstairs, then. Their bedrooms.

They weren't there, either.

Laura's heart was pounding and her hands were icy. Through the tall windows at the end of the hall she could see Sharon Scott's tiny figure. She had turned onto the road.

Alone. The papers hadn't been a ruse, then. But where were Emily and Becky? Had they gone to Nanfran's?

Or had they ever come into the house at all?

The door had never slammed.

Emily's eyes, so anguished, so uncertain. Becky's tears. And I sent them away, Laura thought frantically. I couldn't talk to Sharon in front of them but how could they understand that? All they understood was that I sent them away.

She ran down the stairs again and threw the papers on the dining room table and went out the back door. The stable and the stable yard were empty. Penny and Keno were grazing at the far end of the little attached paddock. Penny lifted her head and whickered a greeting.

Pegasus and Snickers were nowhere to be seen. Their tack was gone.

Nanfran's, then. If they were going to run away... Something stirred at the back of her mind but it was gone before she could catch it. If they were going to run away of course they would have ridden to Nanfran's.

"Penny," Laura called. "Quick, Penny. Let's go."

The mare trotted across the paddock. Laura ran back into the stable for tack. As she tightened the girth she glanced up at the sky. Some clouds. Not that bad, not yet. No time to change into riding tights and boots. She caught the stirrup with the toe of her old running shoe and vaulted up into the saddle.

"Now, Penny," she said, and dug in her heels. Penny, surprised and indignant at such unnecessarily crude behavior, tossed her head and cantered out of the yard.

Eleanor Kinnard had just picked up her pen to sign the first of the papers when Christina Jaramillo tapped on the conference room door.

"Excuse me," she said formally. "Mr. Rafland? Mrs. Rafland is on the phone."

Nick frowned. "You'll have to take a message," he said.

Tina flushed a little at his peremptory tone but held her ground. "She insists on talking to you," she said. "She says it's urgent."

For Tina to interrupt him at all was unusual. For her to persist was unheard-of. Something was wrong. Nick stood up.

"Would you give me a few minutes, Eleanor?" he said. "Is there anything I can get for you? Fresh coffee?"

Eleanor lifted the point of the pen from the paper with a little moue of vexation. "I'll just wait," she said. "I would think that this particular moment would be more important to you, Nick Rafland, than a phone call from that wife of yours."

"Forgive me," Nick said quietly. "This moment is exceedingly important to me, as you very well know. I'll be back in a minute."

"I'm sorry, Nick," Tina said as they walked down the hall. "She just—"

"I'm the one who should apologize," Nick said. "I'm sorry I snapped at you. Is Laura all right? Has something—"

"It's not Laura," Tina said. "It's your mother."

He went into his office. The sky outside the windows was dark, and there were occasional flickers of lightning away to the west. It was impossible, of course, but Nick thought he could feel a breath of the cold stormy air inside the room, at the back of his neck. He picked up the phone. "Nanfran?" he said. "The girls?"

"Emily and Becky are all right," Nanfran said. "I'm at your house out here at the ranch, and they're here with me. It's Laura I'm worried about."

"Laura? Why?"

"Sharon Scott was here. Just after lunch."

Nick stood very still. The sky seemed to be getting blacker. "What happened?" he said.

"A couple of hours ago Laura rode over to my house. She was looking for the girls. I hadn't seen them. She told me that Sharon Scott had just appeared out of nowhere and given her the signed adoption papers and left."

"The papers? Signed?"

"Signed. I have them right here in my hand. Anyway, whatever happened between Laura and Sharon, the girls saw part of it and it upset them. From what they've told me themselves they were already in a state over some tomfoolery Derek said to them about bedrooms. Laura found the ponies gone and thought they'd run away to me."

"Wait a minute. Slow down. Are they with you or aren't they?"

"They are now. They weren't then. And before I could stop her she was off to look for them."

"You should have called me, for God's sake."

"And what would you have done, Nicholson, that Laura wasn't already doing?" Nanfran demanded tartly. "The girls did come here about half an hour after Laura left. They'd decided to run away, all right, but when they saw the weather turning bad they had the good sense to turn around and run straight back home. But Laura's still out there somewhere. She doesn't know they're safe, and she'll ride herself and that mare you bought her right into the ground before she'll give up looking for them."

"I'll be there in an hour," Nick said.

In the conference room Eleanor Kinnard was still toying with her pen. The paper on top of the stack was still unsigned. None of the other papers had been touched. "Eleanor," Nick said. "I'm very sorry, but I'm going to have to go."

Eleanor put the pen down. It made an angry little click on the polished wood of the table. "Go?" she said. "You can't be serious."

"I am serious," Nick said. "I'm sorry. Laura is missing."

"Oh, rubbish," Eleanor said pettishly. "What do you mean, missing? She's a grown woman, and I daresay she can take care of herself. If you leave this meeting now, Nick

Rafland, I am not going to go through all this again. I will never sell you this land. What do you think of that?"

Nick took a single deep breath. Another hour, two perhaps, to complete all the signing and notarizing with the antiquated formality that Eleanor Kinnard demanded. An hour, two perhaps, with Laura somewhere out in the storm alone.

The Black Moon, his life, his dream, his heritage, on one side of the balance.

Laura, on the other.

Laura, teaching Emmie and Becky to eat ice cream cones. Laura on Penny, turning Snickers back at the very brink of the bluff. Laura in one of his old sweatshirts, asleep in his bed. Laura in floating chiffon, all colors of violet, wearing Harriet Nicholson's necklace. Laura, standing in the front hallway just last night...

The truth is that you don't love me and you've never loved me....

Laura.

His heart actually stopped for a moment. His breath stopped. Everything stopped. When it started again he felt as if he'd come out of some long solitary darkness into the light. The conference room was done in unobtrusive greens and grays, but even so the colors hurt his eyes.

The truth, he thought. The truth is that I do love her and I've always loved her and I've been a fool. A fool. A blind quixotic *fool*...

"I'm sorry, Eleanor," he said again. "Mrs. Jaramillo will call your driver for you."

Unexpectedly Eleanor Kinnard laughed. "I never thought I'd see the day," she said mockingly. "And I must say it's just about worth this piddling little piece of land to me. You, Nick, you arrogant black-haired Rafland scoundrel, at the beck and call of a woman. I only wish Jack had been more like you. Willing to give up everything, throw everything away. And all for..."

Nick didn't hear the rest of it. The conference room door swung shut behind him.

Nanfran was waiting at the house, with Keno saddled. "I've packed a lamp and some extra blankets," she said. "First aid kit. Brandy. Some food. And the phone. If either Laura or Penny... Well, you can call me."

It was just starting to rain, slow sullen drops the size of half-dollars. "It's going to rain like hell in a few minutes," Nick said. He had changed into jeans and boots, an old waterproof canvas duster and his weathered Stetson. "Not very good tracking weather. Do you have any idea where she might have gone?"

"The girls said they started for the old homestead," Nanfran said. "But when the weather got so bad they lost their nerve and came back."

If I ever run away from home, Becky had announced that first Saturday, the day of the trail ride, *I'm going to live in the bunkhouse. Just me and nobody else.*

And Laura had been there. *That sounds kind of lonesome,* she had said. *Nobody to care about you, and nobody for you to care about....*

"The old homestead," Nick said. "Of course. That's where she has to be. That's where it finally has to end."

Nanfran caught at his wrist. "End?" she said sharply. "What on earth are you talking about?"

Leather creaked, and Nick was in the saddle. Lightning flickered. Keno sidestepped, switching his tail. The very air seemed green and gray and black. "Nothing," Nick said. "Don't worry. I'll find her."

Chapter Eleven

It had taken four hours to reach the site of the old house on that leisurely Saturday morning with the girls. Rain and all, Nick was there in an hour, soaking wet, Keno trembling with exhaustion and excitement under him. The storm seemed to have settled itself directly overhead, and the wind was driving the rain down in slanting gray sheets. No trace of Penny or Laura. Nick muttered an epithet under his breath.

"All right," he said to the big gelding. "I know. Just a little longer. We'll circle from here."

If she hadn't come here, of course, she could be anywhere. If something had happened to either one of them, it could be days... The position of the foundation stones gave him his bearings. Start quartering the area, then, north to south, east to west. Brush and trees thick around it, hiding God only knew what. Impossible to track in the rain, so listen, listen...

Keno heard it first. The gelding's head came up and his ears pricked, and automatically Nick held him still. Very faintly, it came again. A horse whinnying, shrill fear in the sound.

Penny.

Nick whistled. The mare responded, whinnying again, the sound a little different now, almost humanly anxious. It was Penny. He could hear her thrashing around in the brush. A flash of russet, bedraggled and rain-darkened, and she was there, crowding up against Keno, alone and afraid and desperate for companionship.

Empty saddle.

And so where was Laura?

That was easy. She was somewhere out in the storm, on foot, still looking for the girls. And now looking for Penny as well.

He took Penny back to the clearing and tied her to a sapling on the east side of the bunkhouse, where there was at least a bit of shelter. "Sorry, girl," he said. "I need to keep you in one place for now. I'll be back." The mare whinnied unhappily after him as he urged Keno back into the crisscross quartering pattern. Somewhere out there in the storm...

He had covered almost all of the rise and was beginning to think grimly that he was going to have to start the whole pattern over again when Laura appeared so suddenly out of the rain that he almost rode over her. Obviously he had startled her as much as her abrupt appearance had frightened him, because she lurched back and half fell onto one knee.

"Penny," she said. She staggered to her feet and reached out to the horse. "Oh, God, no. Keno." Then she looked up, her face white, her eyes frantic, the light brown silk of her hair clinging in dark wet ribbons to the delicate shape of her skull. All she had on were jeans and running shoes and a thin short-sleeved white T-shirt with bluebonnets printed across the front. Her bare arms were covered with a bloody network of scratches.

"Nick," she said. She sounded as if she'd seen a man from Mars.

"Come on," he said, over the pounding of the rain. "Damn it, Laura, I was worried sick about you." He held out one hand. "Climb up."

She stepped back. "No," she said. "The girls are out here somewhere. And Penny's..."

The relentless rain and the wind drowned out the rest of the sentence. "Laura," he said. "The girls are safe at home. And I've got Penny back at the bunkhouse."

Apparently she couldn't hear him, either. She turned away and started into the brush again. He dug in his heels and Keno crashed after her. When he drew alongside her he dropped the reins on the gelding's neck and reached down to take hold of her arm.

"Let *go* of me," she screamed. "Don't you understand? The girls are out here. I am not going to leave them."

He got his hands under her arms and lifted her. It wasn't really that cold, but the wind was high and she'd been wet through for so long that she felt as if she'd just surfaced from the depths of the lake. *My lovely water-wife*... As he pulled her across the saddle in front of him she twisted violently in his grasp, clawing at his wrists, her face streaming with rain and tears. Wildly she struck at his face, scratching his cheek, knocking his hat off. She opened her mouth to scream at him, choked on the rain and started to cough.

"Laura," he said. "For the love of God. The girls are *safe*. It's all right."

He wasn't sure if she understood him or not. As gently as he could he pinned her flailing arms against his chest. God, she was cold, shaking so uncontrollably, coughing and sobbing. He held her tightly, trying to warm her. His own face was wet, too, unprotected under the rain and the wind. When she quieted a little he picked up Keno's reins and turned back to the bunkhouse.

* * *

It was warm and dry in the blankets. The blankets were soft. Her arms burned. The rain was still thrumming overhead. Laura curled up with her knees under her chin and ran her hands thoughtfully along her calves. Good heavens. Nothing but skin. What had happened to her clothes? And there was something that she really should be doing, something desperately important. Something about the rain. Something about...

The girls. Penny. Oh, God, and Nick was in it somehow, too.

She sat up suddenly. She was wrapped in clean blankets on an old wooden bunk. There was nothing but blackness outside the tiny windows. A single beam of light sliced through the interior of the bunkhouse, close to the floor, thick with motes of dust. On the other side of the light, Penny and Keno stood quietly, unsaddled, rubbed down, dry, cared-for. The two horses looked unnaturally huge in the small space. Penny turned and looked at her and blew out her breath gently.

The light came from a square red Coleman lamp. Next to it, sitting on the floor under the window with his back against the wall, was her husband.

Not a Nick she ever remembered seeing before. He was wearing jeans muddy to the knees and a shirt that was creased and streaked with rain and mud and exertion. His heavy black hair was wet and ruffled. There was a scratch on his cheek. He was watching her silently, and his oblique dark eyes were tired and still.

What on earth...?

It all came back in a rush. Sharon Scott. Emily's anguished eyes. That heart-stopping moment in the empty house when she had realized that the girls were gone. Riding to Nanfran's, and then on to the site of the old homestead, wrong turns, panic, the rising wind. Penny waiting outside the bunkhouse, startled into flight by a sudden crack of thunder. Searching, calling, frenziedly tearing her way through the brush, until suddenly and shockingly Nick and Keno had loomed up out of the rain. Screaming and fighting and clawing like a wild thing . . .

"Nick?" she whispered. He simply looked at her. She cleared her throat. "I scratched you," she said. "Oh, Nick, I'm sorry."

One corner of his mouth turned down very slightly. It was not exactly a smile. "This time," he said, "you did faint."

"Did I?" she said. "I remember . . . I remember fighting and screaming like a madwoman. I didn't realize... You said the girls had come home?"

"Yes."

"Are they all right?"

"Yes."

She swallowed. "Are you all right?" she said.

"I'm fine."

"Nanfran." She swung her legs over the edge of the bed, trying to wrap one of the blankets around her naked body. "Oh, Nick, she'll be frantic. Where are my clothes? We have to—"

"Don't worry," he said. "I called her. I brought the phone when I came after you."

"Did she tell you about the papers? About Sharon Scott?"

"She told me."

He paused. Nicholson Rafland, the articulate, the confident, the casual master of the well-turned phrase, apparently couldn't think of anything else to say. He sat there, disheveled, scratched, tired, vulnerable, at a loss for words. Completely un-Nick-like. Her heart contracted.

"You were supposed to be at your meeting," she said at last. "Your meeting with Eleanor Kinnard."

"I left."

"What did she say?"

"That if I left she wouldn't meet with me again."

"*What?*"

He smiled very faintly, a ghost of his characteristic self-mocking grin. "Enjoy being here while you can," he said. "We'll never come back. This will never be Rafland land again. At least not in my lifetime."

"But you said she was ready to sign the deeds. That she was going to bring her lawyers with her and everything."

"Oh, they were all there. She had the pen in her hand. Quite literally. Then Nanfran called."

"You should have *stayed,*" Laura said passionately. "I would have been all right. Oh, Nick, that's not *fair.* It was the one thing in the world you wanted."

"No," he said. "It was the one thing in the world I thought I wanted."

He stopped again. Laura could think of nothing more to say. Then she saw him swallow. He stood up and took two steps and sat down beside her on the bunk. It creaked under his weight. He lifted his hands and laid them gently on either side of her face.

"Laura," he said. His voice was soft and shaky. "It was you. When it came down to a choice I realized it was you I really wanted. You I really... Oh, God, Laura. I should have known the night of the dance. It was good to see Julie and talk to her and know that she was happy. But it was you I wanted to be with. You I wanted to touch. You."

She stared at him. "Me," she repeated.

"From the beginning," he said. "Nanfran's been right all along, and I was just too blind to see it. Too blind to see my own romantic posturing."

"Nick. I'm not sure... What are you trying to say to me?"

"Now and always," he said softly. "You. Only you. I love you, Laura."

The words hung in the air. The rain had settled into a steady patter against the roof. The horses were drowsing, breathing softly. For what seemed like forever there was no motion, nothing but sound.

His shirt was buttoned all the way to the throat against the rain and the chill. Slowly Laura reached out and unbuttoned the first button. Then she unbuttoned two more and rested her forehead against the warm little triangle of skin between the points of his collarbones. He smelled of rain and leather and the horses and himself, of effort and tension and love.

"Not just words?" she said.

"Not just words."

"Nick?"

"Mmm?"

"Put your arms around me."

He did. At first he held her very gently, but when she lifted her own arms and wrapped them around his neck his embrace closed around her, hard and fervent. "Laura," he said. His voice was very soft and husky. "My sweetheart. My Amazon."

She kissed him. Around his mouth the skin was prickly with the beginning of stubble. His arms were hard under the soft cloth of his shirt. She shivered a little and pressed against him.

"Nick?" she said. "Are we going to stay here all night?"

"We don't have much choice, unless you want to go back out in the rain."

"No," she said. "I don't want to go back out in the rain. But I worked all morning, moving my things into your bedroom."

His head came up fractionally. After a moment a smile twitched at one corner of his mouth. "Well," he said, "I suppose we could pretend we were there."

"I suppose we could."

"It would certainly resolve the question once and for all."

"What question?"

"Of whether we're really married or not."

"If we're going to be really married," Laura said, "I don't think it's fair that I'm the only one with no clothes on."

"How very odd, Mrs. Rafland."

"Odd?"

"I was just thinking the same thing."

He stood up. She closed her eyes and thought about clothes. Nicholson Rafland, that first day at the Driskill, a stranger, so formidable in his immaculately tailored dark gray suit. Nick kneeling by Yegua Creek in faded jeans and a scarlet cotton shirt, wreathed in wildflowers. Nick at the Hyatt, turning heads from one end of the ballroom to the other in his severely elegant black and white. Whatever he wore, he always seemed to fit so faultlessly into his clothes. And now...

The old bunk shifted under his weight. Without opening her eyes she moved, turned toward him, and all of a sudden he was holding her in the cocoon of blankets, naked skin against naked skin. It was more of a shock that she had ever thought it could be. She gasped and clutched at him almost as if she were falling.

"Shh," he said. "Ah, God, Laura, you don't know how much I've wanted to hold you like this." He kissed her temple, and then caught her hair in one hand and slowly pulled her head back so that he could reach her mouth.

Her soft exhalation of pleasure was lost in the kiss, in the feel and the taste of his lips and the slow quizzical heat of his tongue rediscovering her mouth. She clung to his shoulders, feeling the soft prickle of black hair at the back of his neck, the surprising smoothness of his skin and the heavy fluid shift of the muscles beneath it. After a long time he lifted his head.

"How lovely you are," he said. His hand moved, the palm caressing. She felt her flesh contract, while at the same time its sensitivity expanded, flowering into his touch. Involuntarily she sucked in her breath and arched her back, pressing up against him. He moved his hand again. Sensation flared, and all of a sudden she could feel the hot blood pulsing in her body, defining nerves she never knew she had, secret hollows, and all the warm silky places where her flesh folded together.

"Do you like that, then?" he said, his voice very close to her ear. "Tell me, sweetheart."

Laura swallowed. How swollen her throat seemed to be. "Yes," she managed to whisper. "I like that."

He kissed her ear, and the point of her jaw, and her collarbone. She tightened her arms around his neck again, and pressed her face against his shoulder. A little speculatively she opened her mouth against his skin: heat and a sheen of dampness and the taste of soap and salt and wildness.

"Oh, Nick," she said. "Oh, please..."

He moved against her, leaned over her. Shyly, with a sense of something almost like formality, she embraced him, felt the tense powerful muscles of his chest and stomach, his long legs, strong and warm. His unfamiliar shape against her own smooth softness. She trembled and turned her face away.

"Oh, no," he said. "Look at me, Laura."

She hesitated, tears hot in her eyes. But at last she looked up at him.

"Light in darkness," he said softly. "My heart. My love."

She shut her eyes. He moved. Then he was still for a moment, his breathing uneven, his head bowed against her shoulder.

"Laura?" he said.

"It's all right," she whispered. "Oh, Nick, I never dreamed..."

He moved again, a little quicker and harder. She cried out in surprise and the beginning of delight. He lifted his head and kissed her mouth, and she felt the muscles in his arms contract. His weight withdrew, leaving a surprising emptiness behind.

"Oh, no," she said. "Don't. Don't..."

He moved, obliterating the emptiness with a ravishing little shock. She gasped and clutched at his shoulders, his back. He pulled away again and she tensed, knowing now what was coming, waiting, shivering, and just when she thought she could bear it no longer he moved again, deep and sudden and sure. Pleasure exploded, flaming instantaneously from the center of her body to the furthest tips of a hundred different nerves.

"Nick," she gasped. "I love you. Always. Always. Oh, Nick, I love you so much."

He murmured something against her ear, her name, an endearment, a question, but all her senses were intent on some vaulting mysterious extremity and the words themselves were lost. She felt her whole body tightening, closing in around him, encircling him. *Mine,* she thought fiercely, with a sudden blaze of sheer primitive possessiveness. Now and forever, *mine*...

The sound of the rain closed in around them. He gave himself up to her, utterly and completely. And little by little she followed him, outside time, outside thought, from the beginning of delight all the way through to the end.

At dawn he woke her.

"Nick," she said drowsily. "Oh, Nick, I love you."

"I love you, too, sweetheart," he said softly. "Come on, get dressed. Are you hungry?"

"Do you have food?"

"I don't know. But Nanfran packed my saddlebags, so there's probably a six-course dinner in there with four forks for each of us. Get dressed first, and we'll eat on the way."

He coaxed the horses out of the bunkhouse and saddled them while she pulled on her wrinkled, muddy jeans and T-shirt. Good heavens, what a scarecrow pair we are, she thought. But how happy I am. How happy I am.

She walked out into the morning. Every cloud had vanished and the sky was pink and gold and a milky moonstone blue. Nick slapped Penny's chestnut haunch and turned.

"Ready?" he said.

"Ready."

"Let me help you."

Demurely Laura allowed him to lift her into the saddle. Although it wasn't entirely demureness. Swinging up onto the back of a horse, she thought, isn't exactly what I would have chosen to do this morning. All things considered.

He smiled at her. "How very un-Amazon-like you are this morning, Mrs. Rafland," he said. "We'll take our time. And if you want to stop, just say so."

"What I want," she said, "is for you to see what Nanfran packed in those saddlebags."

Two oranges and a box of granola bars. Not exactly a six-course meal, but welcome enough if you hadn't eaten since noon the day before. When Laura bit down on the first crescent-shaped section of orange the juice burst into her mouth, clean and tart and exhilarating.

"Nick?" she said, when they'd been riding for a while.

"Hmm?"

"Tell me about my father. What he said to you."

He glanced over at her thoughtfully. "Are you sure you wouldn't rather talk to him yourself? When you're ready?"

"No. I don't mind anymore. That you talked to him, I mean. I just want to know. I saw all those notes you made but I don't remember exactly what they said."

"He's an artist," Nick said. "An impressionist. All his life he's worked ordinary jobs just to give himself time to paint."

"So you were right. Sensuous, spontaneous, creative, all those things you said."

"I was right," Nick said, "in more ways than one."

It was really a little late to be blushing at anything Nick said, but Laura felt the heat rising in her cheeks anyway. She looked away. "How did he meet my mother?"

"He was working on her house. Some kind of carpentry, apparently. It was right around Christmas and both of them were alone. Both of them were lonely. Holidays are hard sometimes."

"But why didn't she just *marry* him?"

"He was younger than she was," Nick said. "Ten years younger. And he was a carpenter. Even worse, an artist. Not the kind of person a Gardiner married. He says he tried. She wouldn't talk to him on the telephone and she sent his letters back. Finally he just gave up."

"Did he ever . . . well, suspect? About me?"

"No. He didn't even know she'd adopted a child. They weren't exactly in the same social circles. And for whatever it may be worth, he doesn't 'drink alcohol to excess.'"

Laura frowned. "How on earth do you know that?" she demanded.

"He told me. He wanted to know how I'd gotten his name after all this time, and I told him a little bit about the letter."

"Can we still go? To Charleston, I mean, next week."

"If you want to. He did marry eventually, you know. You have a brother. A half brother, at least. Two half sisters. You even have a baby niece of your own."

Laura closed her eyes against sudden hot tears. "Oh, Nick," she said. "I'm so sorry about your land. That's the only thing that didn't work out, isn't it? Everything else we got married for . . . We have Emily and Becky safe. I found out...found out how my mother felt about me, and who my father is. It doesn't seem right that you shouldn't have the land you wanted so much."

He edged Keno closer and took her hand in his. "I found something I wanted even more," he said. He kissed her fingertips very lightly. "Look. We're almost home. And I think we're about to have a rather boisterous welcome."

Across the meadow Laura could see the two ponies, one chocolate-colored, one snowy white. They were galloping as hard as their fat little legs could carry them. "Becky better not let him run away with her this morning," Laura said. "I don't think I'm up to any equestrian heroics just at the moment."

"Let's stop, then," he said. "And let them come to us."

He helped her down. For a moment he simply held her, his body strong and familiar behind hers, his head bent, his unshaven cheek warm against her temple.

"Tell me," he said softly. "Tell me one more time."

Laura let her head drop back against his shoulder. "I love you, Nick," she said.

Then the girls were there, flinging themselves down from their ponies, clamoring to be hugged and kissed and listened to. Laura caught them up in her arms, laughing. Nick opened his arms, too, and somehow managed to encompass all three of them.

Something like light leaped in a circle around them. Kinship. Belonging. Love. All intertwined. And all real. Never again anything make-believe, Laura thought, in a flash of joy and gratitude and fulfillment that closed her throat and blinded her eyes. Never a make-believe mom. Never a make-believe daughter. And never, never a make-believe wife...

"Mom moved all her things into your room, Uncle Nick," Becky was saying accusingly. "And then you didn't even come home. I don't think you're ever going to be really married."

"They'll be really married tonight," Emily said in her soft serious voice. "Won't you, Aunt Laura? Uncle Nick? The two of you, together?"

"Yes," Laura said. "Yes, my honey, we will. We'll be together, tonight and every other night. I promise."

"And of course you always..." Nick murmured, "always...*always* keep your promises."

* * * * *

Silhouette ROMANCE™

COMING NEXT MONTH

#1138 A FATHER FOR ALWAYS—Sandra Steffen

Fabulous Fathers

To keep his daughter, single dad Jace McCall needed a fake fiancée—fast! So when he asked Garret Fletcher to be his pretend bride, Garret couldn't refuse. After all, she didn't have to pretend she was in love....

#1139 INSTANT MOMMY—Annette Broadrick

Daughters of Texas/Bundles of Joy

Widowed dad Deke Crandal knew horses and cattle—not newborn baby girls! So how could Mollie O'Brien resist Deke's request for help? Especially when she secretly wished to be a permanent part of the family.

#1140 WANTED: WIFE—Stella Bagwell

Lucas Lowrimore was ready to settle down—with Miss Right. He just didn't expect to fall for pretty police officer Jenny Prescott. She was definitely the wife he wanted, but Jenny proved to be a hard woman to win!

#1141 DEPUTY DADDY—Carla Cassidy

The Baker Brood

Carolyn Baker had to save her orphaned godchildren from their uncle, Beau Randolf! What would a single farmer know about *twin* infants? But Beau wasn't the greenhorn Carolyn had expected!

#1142 ALMOST MARRIED—Carol Grace

Laurie Clayton thought she'd never love again—until Cooper Buckingham charmed her and the baby she was caring for. Everything seemed perfect when they were together, almost as if they were married! But would Laurie ever be able to take a chance and say, "I do"?

#1143 THE GROOM WORE BLUE SUEDE SHOES—Jessica Travis

With his sensuous sneer and bedroom eyes, Travor Steele was a dead ringer for Elvis Presley. But it was gonna take a whole lotta shakin' to convince Erin Weller that he wasn't the new king—but her next groom!

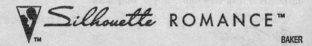

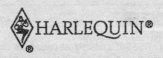

The Perils Of Pink Cat

I was the tiniest *and* **skinniest** *and* **liveliest** kitten from a very large family.

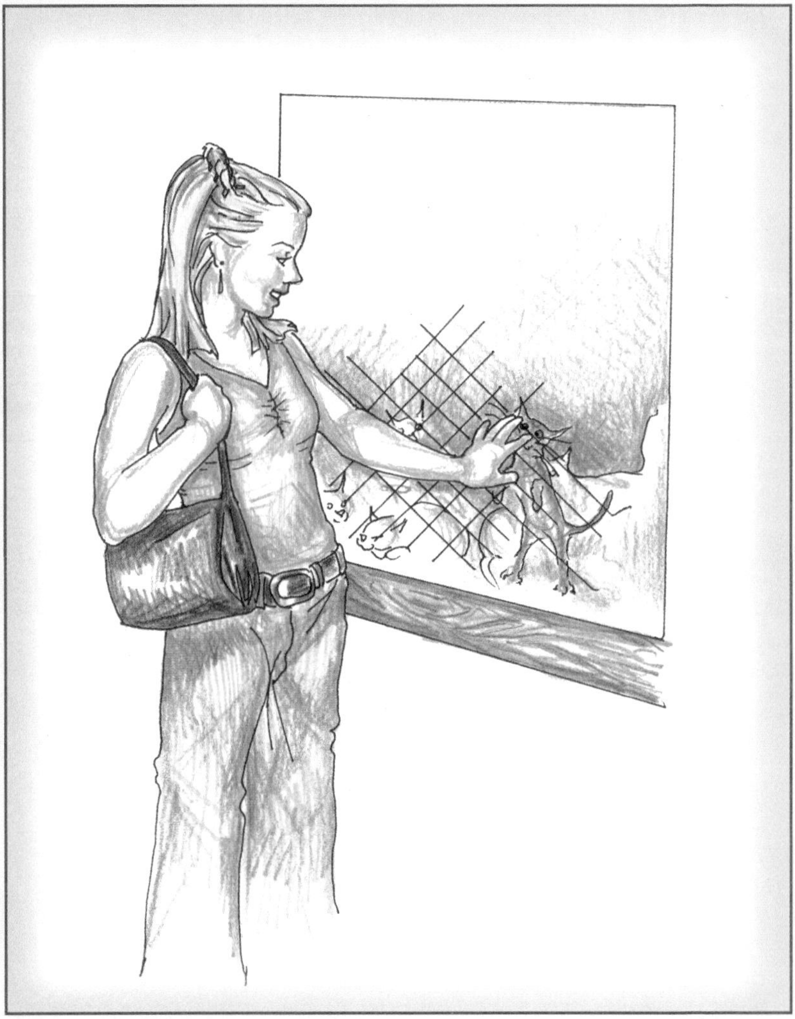

That's what the pretty blonde girl said when she picked me out from the shelter.

For a
brief period,
Eve and I lived
in our own
little universe.
She carried me around
wherever
she went

and
whatever she was
doing.

I loved it.

I thought **that all cats**

lived this way...

Eve couldn't take me with her when she decided to go into the Army, so she loaned me out to her Mom, whose own household was full of all sorts of cats – and a horse, and

two dogs: **Rupert** and **Belle**, and
Stan-Lee the rabbit, and birds, and even
a squirrel named Jedson (for a while),
and on,
and on,
and on!

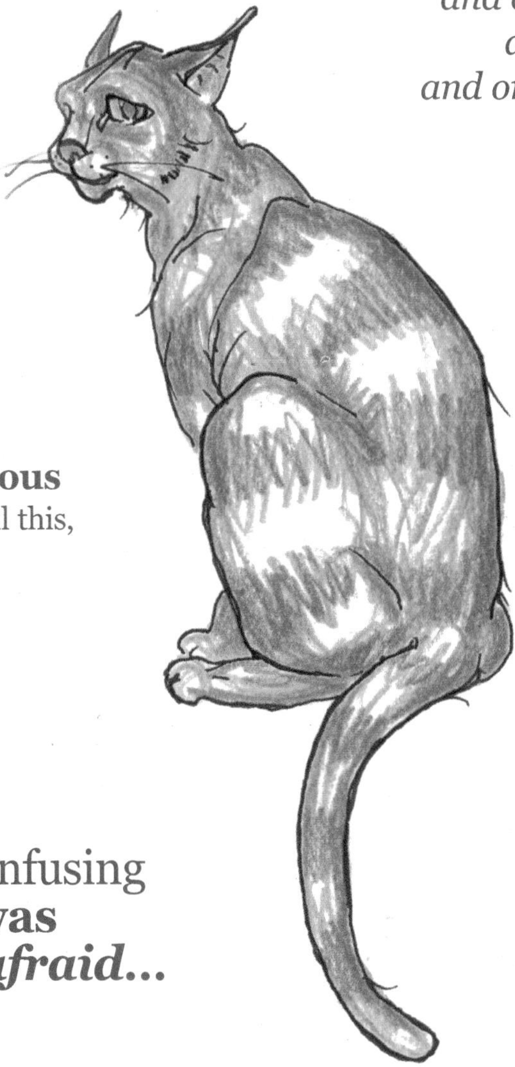

I was curious
about all this,
but it was all

so confusing
and **I was**
so afraid...

At Eve's, I was a pampered **apartment cat**,
so I was delighted to discover the great outdoors here,
and it was tempting
to linger in the wild
past dusk...

One
crisp evening
in the autumn
shortly after my
arrival, I was
totally absorbed
in woods
exploration

when I heard the call to come home,
and inside to safety.

The human voices
grew more urgent, but I
ignored them,
tantalized as I was
by the
shadows

of sunset on the branches,
and the rustling of skinks and mice
in the leaves...

I will never know
what it was that
startled me –

perhaps a raccoon,
or even a bloodthirsty pack of coyotes!
The snap of twigs
sent me scrambling up the nearest tree
in a wink.
This particular maple, however, was just like
a telephone pole – very tall, straight
as an arrow, and *without*
a single branch on it **from the ground**
almost to the top...

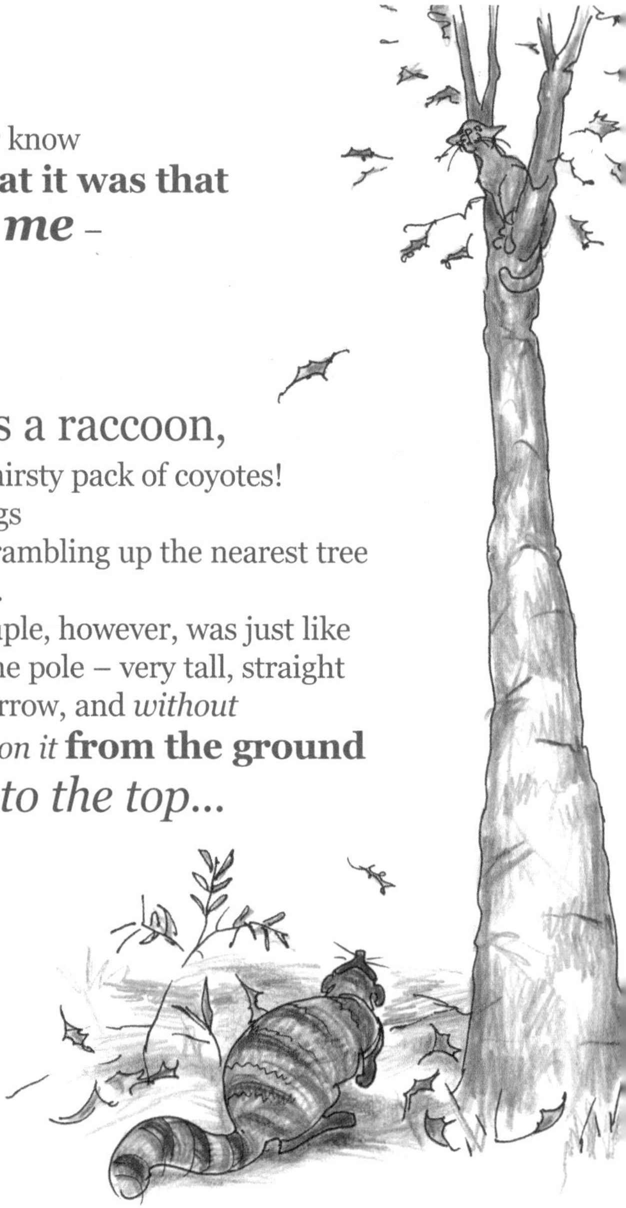

I perched nervously
in a narrow fork,
meowing

and howling to be rescued as the
terrifying darkness closed in.
The humans found me,
and immediately understood
my predicament.
They coaxed me
for hours to come down on my own, *but I
was frozen in fear* and wouldn't be
moved by food or sweet persuasion
of any kind...

"Aw,
he'll come
down
when
he's good and ready –
or if he
gets hungry
enough!"

"You think?

Oh, I certainly hope so," they remarked to each other, trailing one by one back into the house...

Alone*, the chilly night settling in around me,* I shrank from the strange noises and terrible shrieks of woods-dwelling creatures. I thought wistfully of my crunchy dry food, warm bed and the ***welcome stroke of a human hand...***

Morning found me in the same position –

stiff and exhausted from
trying all night to steady my balance.
I resumed my plaintive cries
for help.

Scott, one of the bigger boys,
had driven in
from school late the night before, so at
Mom's insistence he came
out to study my situation. He
promptly and expertly shimmied
up the slender tree,

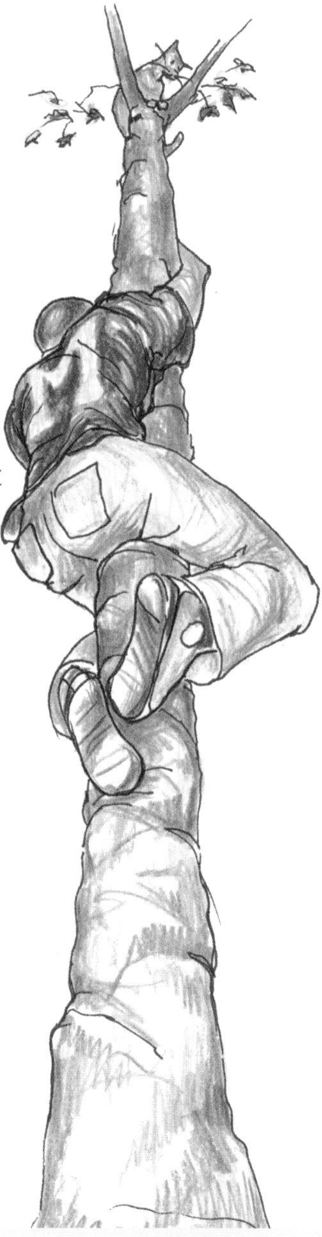

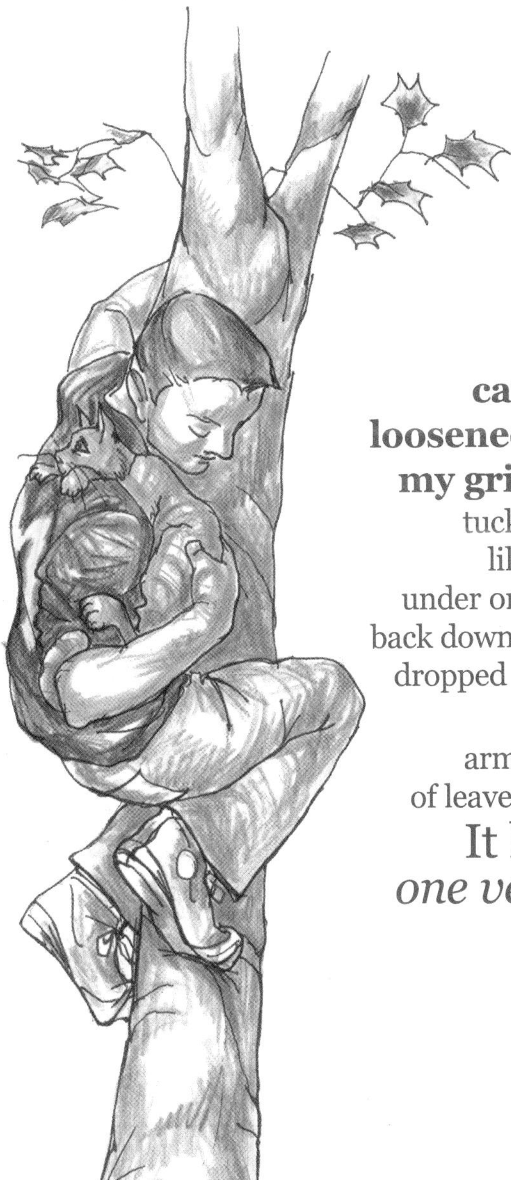

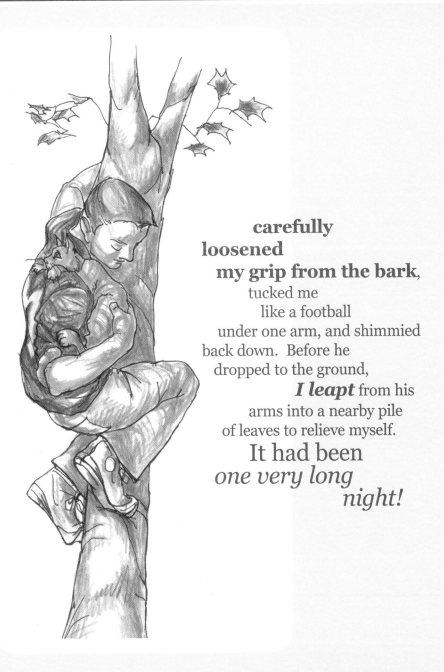

carefully loosened my grip from the bark, tucked me like a football under one arm, and shimmied back down. Before he dropped to the ground, ***I leapt*** from his arms into a nearby pile of leaves to relieve myself.

It had been *one very long night!*

I'm leggy

with a huge, rangy frame, so I might have been mistaken for one tough cookie – **but all I really wanted to do was make friends**. The humans began mocking me right away, and the other cats ***ignored*** my kind gestures and tried to *run me out of town!*

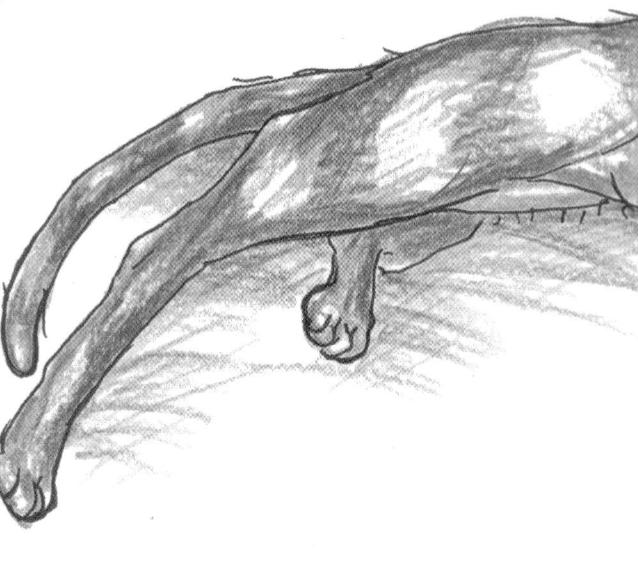

In spite of this,
I have a *forgiving* nature.
I love humans – especially the ladies. As soon as a hand touches my fur, I start in with my rumble-purr.

I just can't help it – *it switches on by itself* automatically. Could that be why everyone thought *I was such a baby?*

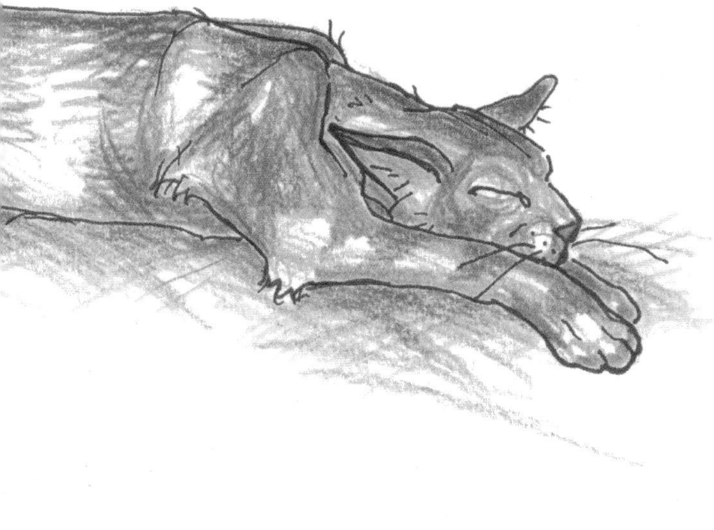

Eve's sister, Mrs. Anderzij, is one of
my very dearest ladyfriend acquaintances.
You can tell she's a cat-person. When she
comes to visit, she
always addresses me with
an affectionate **"Winkles" or "Pinkles".**
I get all trembly inside as I listen
to her velvety voice.

When a human settles down,
and lets me show my love, I start right in
with **"kneading"**, or
working my paws.

I guess my eyes get a little glazed at that point – **it's so wonderful to be loved!** Then I might show them *my stretch*, which can practically reach from one room to another, my body is

s-o-o-o-o
l-o-o-o-ng!

I liked
the little
tabby sisters
(Iris & Olive)
from Day One.
They're twins –
but oh, so different
from each other!
One fat, the other thin, one outgoing,
the other shy – you know how it goes.
They're rather ***smitten* with me, *too,*** and often seek
my company
for snuggling.

It was a hard lesson for me to find out
that you **can't please everyone.**
One of the new guys here –
a big black and white street sport called
Gleb the Terrible – has seen very little handling.
He's companionable enough, but
way too macho for my tastes.
He tries to playfully rough me up
when he's bored
and can't go outside.

I've been told many times
that I don't have a mean bone in my body,
but **there's one cat here**
who most surely DOES.

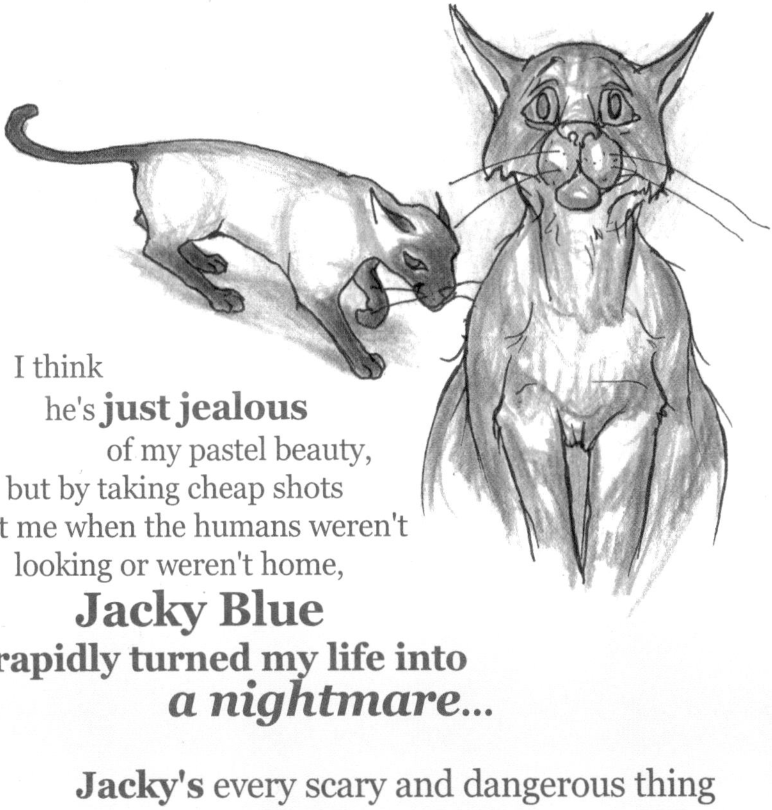

I think
he's **just jealous**
of my pastel beauty,
but by taking cheap shots
at me when the humans weren't
looking or weren't home,
Jacky Blue
rapidly turned my life into
a nightmare...

Jacky's every scary and dangerous thing
I have EVER imagined... I used to
worry constantly about him lurking in shadows or
dark corners, ready to pounce. Even though I outsize him
by a lot, he's **smart**,
quick and
savage.

If I forgot to hide from him,
he would ***nail me***
while I ate, so... I started
wolfing down food as fast
as I could, just in case...
This led to eating
only on the run and
more frequently,
just in case...
which led to eating a little more,
in order to feel better
after having just been
mauled...

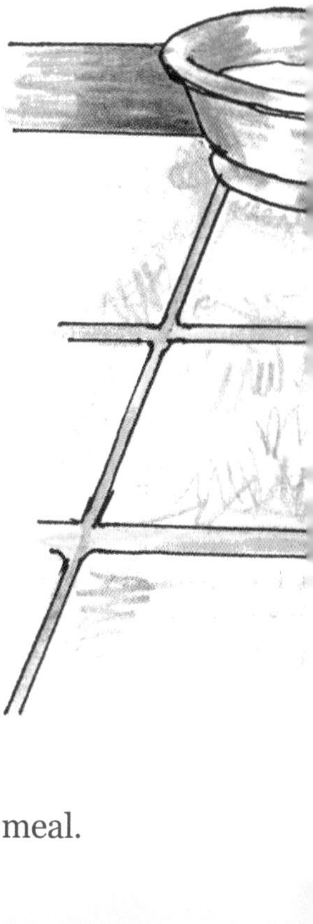

Food
became such **a comfort** to me
in my loneliness, that I was
emptying the bowl several times a day
and still
looking anxiously
toward the next meal.

At first, our humans
couldn't tell why food was
disappearing
so fast
because we all share
the same bowls.

I grew *huge*
and very *fat*.
I didn't care about
going outside
anymore...
I spent my days
(and nights)
lounging
and sleeping...

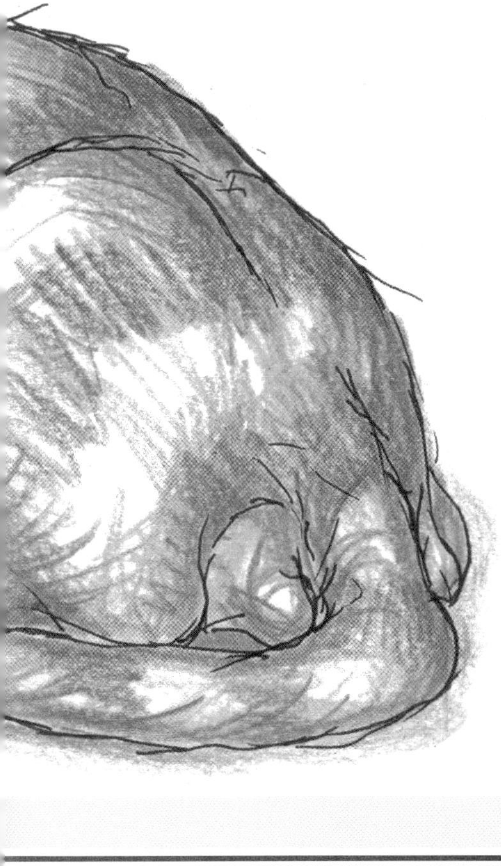

Even the
running
I had to do
to escape my
tormentors
didn't
whittle off
the pounds –
it just made me
eat faster
and more.

The ambushes
increased because
I moved
more slowly
and was easily
captured...
So did
the jokes
about my
weight...

*"Hey, Pink Cat!
Wow, are you
tubby!"*

"Pink Cat's turned into a real lard-belly...why is he eating so much?"

"Gee, Pinkles – slow down! **Stop eating like it's your last meal..."**

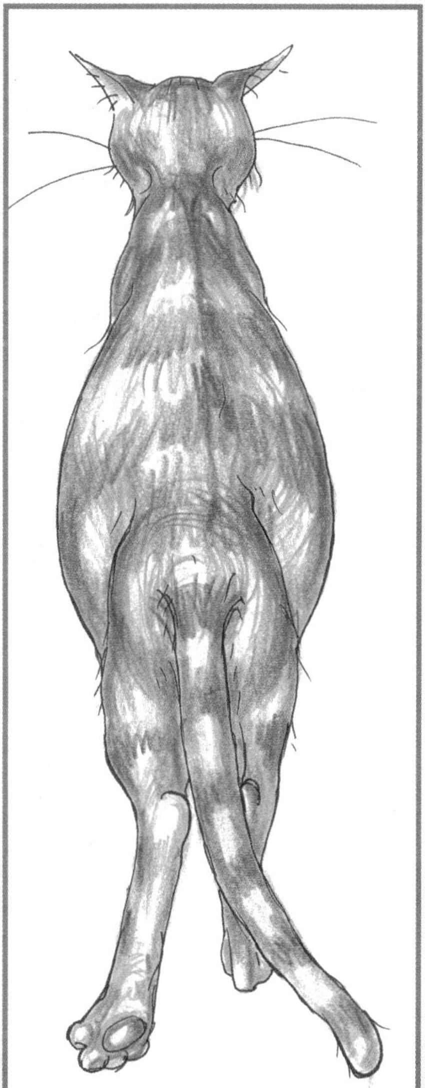

Yes – why was I eating so much?

I simply didn't know... I just felt **lonelier** and **gloomier** with each passing day...

Then, late that summer,
Gleb the Terrible came down with a nasty cold
in spite of his robust constitution –
and which he threw off with ease.
Only **Olive** and **Iris**
managed to escape the runny nose, coughing
and fatigue from that awful bug.
But everyone recovered fully –

except me.
I was
depressed
to begin with,
but now
I didn't even
enjoy eating...

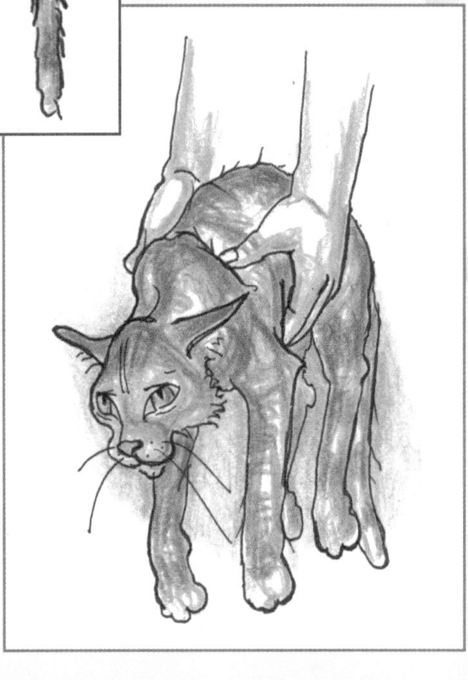

Olive occasionally tried
to lift my spirits,
but I got thinner and weaker,
and **I stopped**
grooming myself...

I would hover over the food bowl
and *just look at* my favorite, crunchy dry food...
I couldn't keep
anything down.

By the time
I went to see Doc,
I had pneumonia and jaundice
and had to stay overnight
at the clinic.
I was so far gone that Doc
summoned my humans
with
those **words**
every pet dreads:

"I think
it's **time**
to do
something
about: Pink Cat

He's/she's not
getting
any better..."

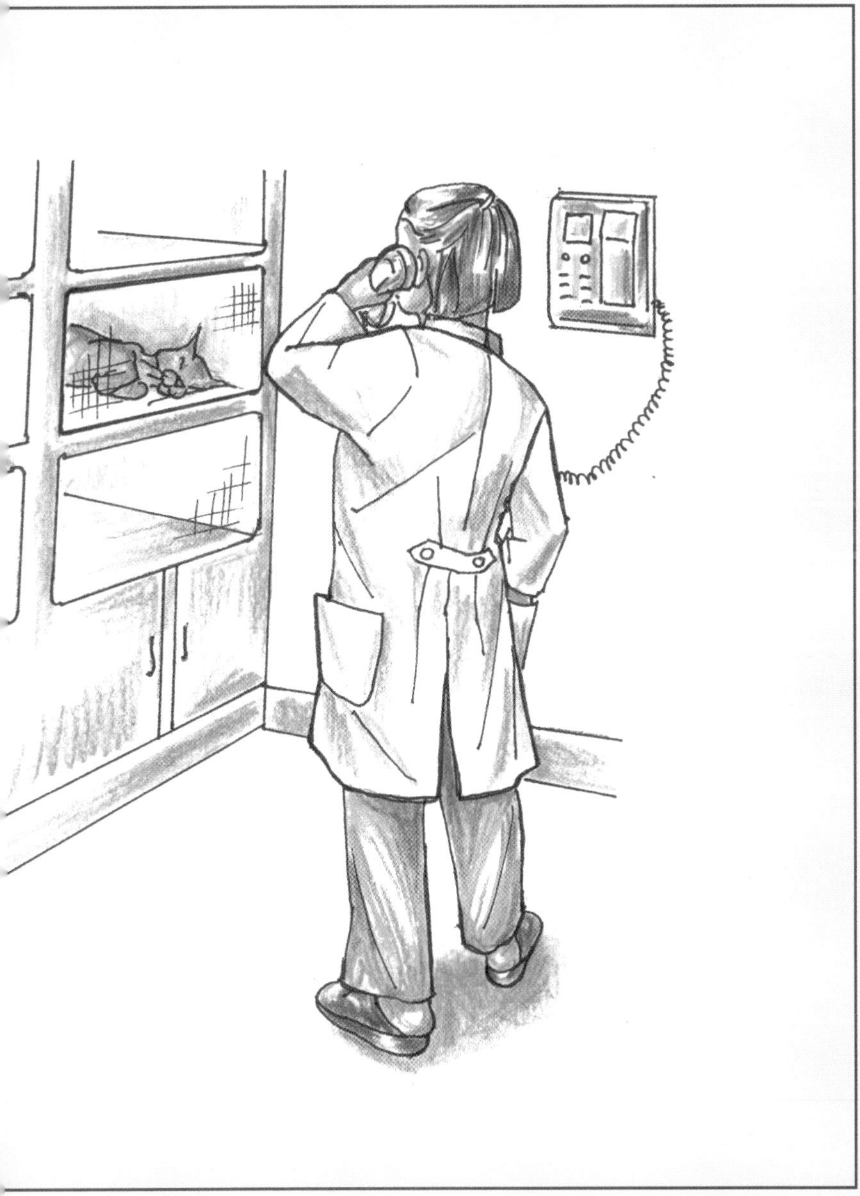

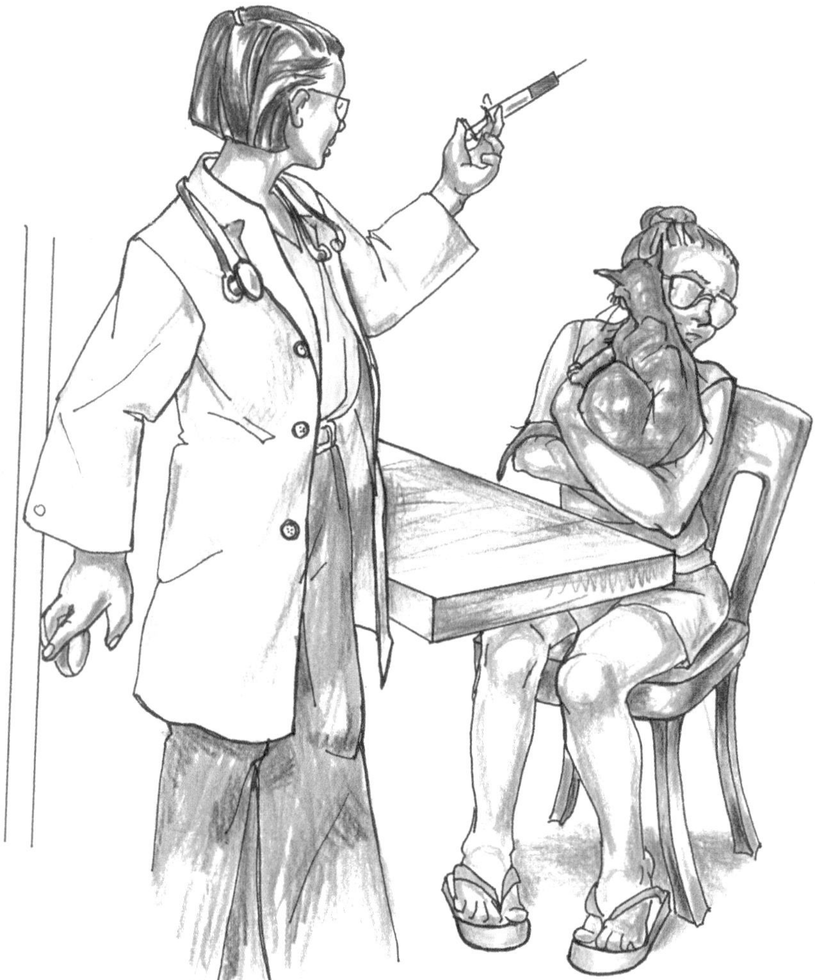

I rallied all my strength
when Mom came
"to get it over with",
dredging up
my final reserves of purr.
I rolled my head against her in a desperate display
of devotion...

She got the message!
When Doc came into the examining room –
syringe in hand
and chock-full of the Potion of Death that would
dispatch me to Cat Heaven –
Mom said,
"I don't think we're going
to put anyone down today,"
and a big tear
trickled down her
cheek...

Doc answered briskly, **"O.K., fine.**
You know, herbal supplements and a special
diet just might give him a chance to recover."

She agreed so cheerfully, I could tell
she was relieved...

It was touch-and-go for a long time...

I still couldn't eat, so I had to be

tube-fed

through the neck

and this didn't always

go smoothly...

sometimes I
puked
it up
right after we
were done...

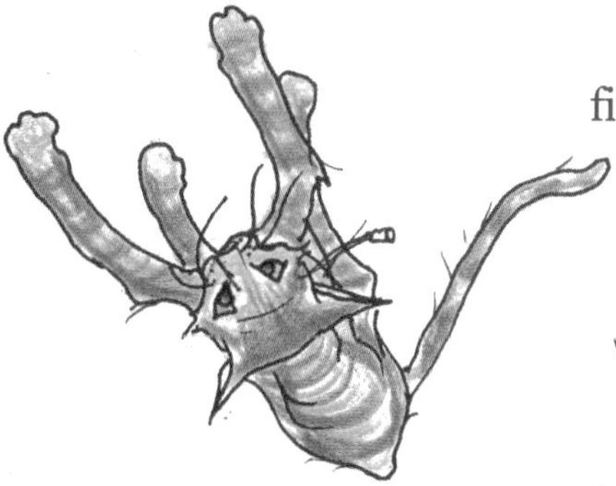

Mom
performed this messy ritual
out on the deck.
Once, when we were
finishing up with the ordeal,
**I staggered over
to the rails.**
I was still weak and
woozy – before she realized it,
I had slipped
through the rails and
dropped right off
the edge...

The fall took forever:
I tumbled over
and over,
and landed
with a soft thud
squarely on top of
Stan-Lee,
grazing
placidly in the
shade
of the catwalk.

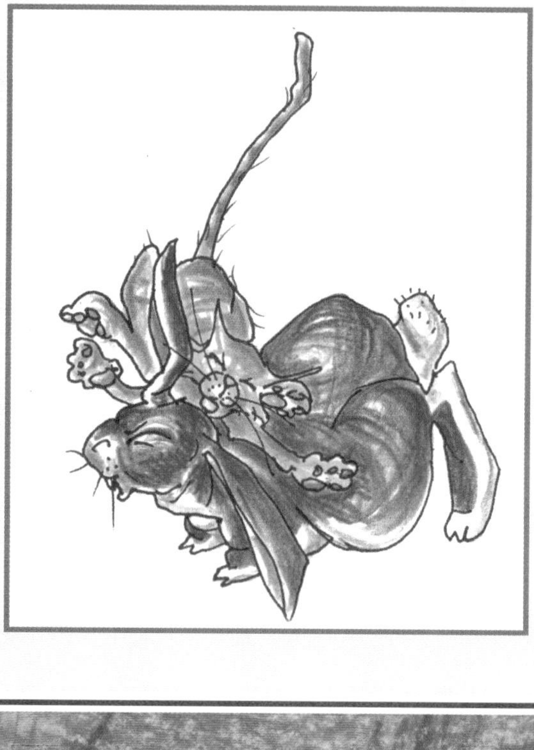

He snorted in indignation as I rolled off, and bounded away, everything intact but his pride.

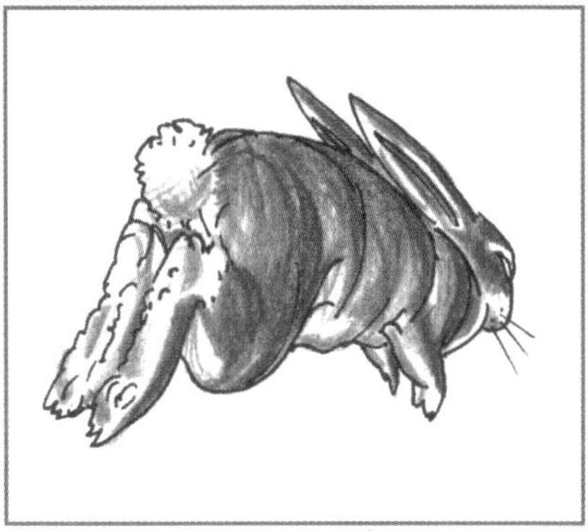

Mom rushed to my side

and gently picked me up. I was dazed, but unhurt – **thanks to a fat bunny cushion** that happened to be in the right place at the right time...

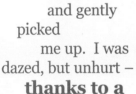

From then on,

I steadily improved,

and now *I am completely restored to health.* I am trim again as well as handsome, with the luxurious lustre back in my pink coat...

***Best of all*, no one picks on me anymore** – cat or person.

Jacky still sulks and threatens, but now that's all he does. If the humans make fun of me, I can feel the love behind it, and they go out of their way to shower me with attention.

I'm truly happy now...

Maybe all the troublemakers regret the cruelty that *put me in peril* in the first place...

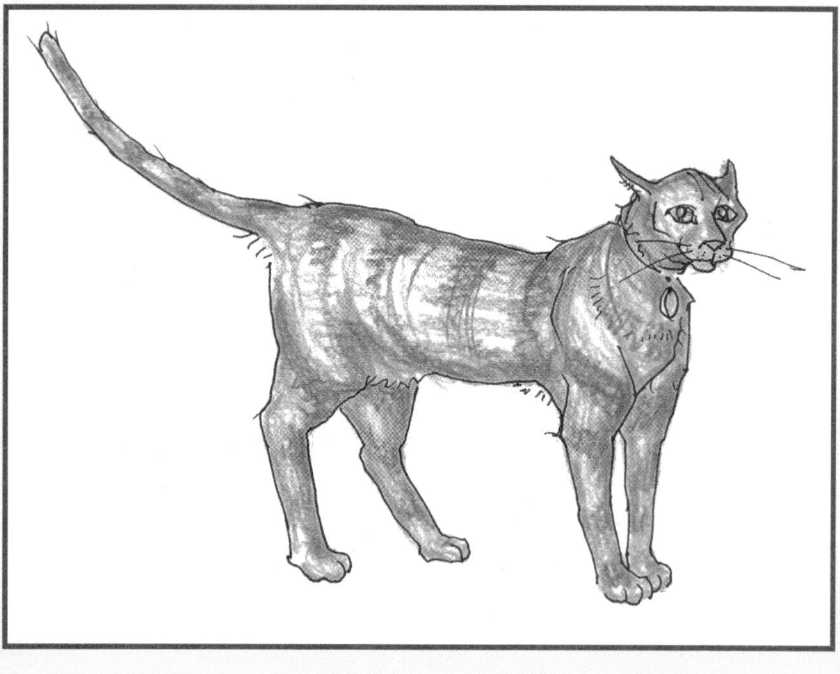